SEALED WITH A BITE

The Nightstar Shifters 3

ARIEL MARIE

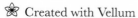

If someone truly loves you, they won't tell you love stories, they will make a love story with you.

unknown

Chapter One

"I was going to pee my pants." Bess giggled.

Adelina Ransome turned and watched her very pregnant sister make her way back to their table. They had attended the wedding of Robin and Heather, two women who had fallen in love. Robin's wolf had identified Heather as her mate, and now everyone was celebrating the human tradition of a wedding and reception.

"Glad you made it," Adelina snickered. She dodged Bess's hand when she took her seat next to her.

"If anything, I would have snuck off in the woods behind a tree and lifted this dress up." Bess laughed.

Adelina tried to imagine Bess doing that and

burst out laughing. Her belly was humongous, and she more than likely would have tipped over trying to squat.

"Addy! Don't laugh. This baby is using my bladder as a pillow and always sending me to the toilet." Bess sighed.

"Well, it won't be too much longer." Addy patted Bess on her shoulder. A pang of jealously ripped through Addy. She glanced around, taking in the party that was in full swing. Music blared through speakers around the outdoor spread.

Everything was decorated beautifully. White-clothed tables with fancy flower centerpieces were placed around the dance floor which was currently filled. The two families hadn't spared any expense when it came to the occasion.

The entire town had shown up for this celebration. The shifters of Howling Valley loved to party. Tasty food, endless drinks and music, was all they needed to have a good time.

Addy tapped her foot to the beat of the music. She reached for her wine glass and took a sip.

"You don't have to sit here with me if you don't want to," Bess announced.

"What are you talking about? I don't mind

keeping you company." Addy held her glass and gave her sister a smile.

"You are single and should be out there, not seated here babysitting your older sister because my ankles are swollen and I'm crabby." Bess pushed her thick hair behind her ear.

They were similar in looks. Both had dark auburn-reddish hair, and the same amber eyes shifters were born with. Most times they were questioned if they were twins, but Bess was older by three years.

Addy, the baby of the family, was the only one single.

Bess and their elder brother, Zeff, had found their mates. Both of them were happily committed to the one person the fates had seen fit to give them. Zeff was mated to Lynne, and they already had a five-year-old son, Junior.

"I'm fine." Addy reached over and squeezed her sister's hand. Her wolf had been mostly quiet since they had arrived at the function. She'd walked through the crowds, stopping to speak with people she knew.

But her wolf hadn't said a word.

It was frustrating being the only one of her

siblings to not be mated. Her parents were constantly reminding her that she wasn't.

According to them, she needed to look harder or find someone where she could mate out of convenience.

But she didn't want to settle.

Adelina Ransome wanted to find her other half.

The one person the fates had chosen for her.

She didn't want to enter a relationship with someone just to have someone. What if she did, had kids, and then boom! Her mate presented themselves.

There had been a few stories of where this had happened. Some worked out fine, while others not so much.

Addy would like to think her wolf would be a jealous bitch when it came to her mate.

Her parents meant well.

Biggs and Clover Ransome wanted all of their children mated off so they could have a ton of grandkids. They were retired and ready for the next stage in their lives.

Spoiling the future generation.

Her parents were afraid she'd end up alone for the rest of her life. They also failed to remember that she was only twenty-nine years old. For shifters, that was still young, but her parents had practically labeled her an old maid.

But in reality, she felt as if her biological clock had officially started ticking.

Shifters were blessed with long lives. Her parents were well into their eighties and didn't look a day over fifty.

Searching for one's mate was not as easy as it sounded. She'd grown up in Howling Valley and had yet to meet anyone who drew her wolf's interest. Maybe her mate wasn't in the area.

What if her mate wasn't a shifter?

Addy didn't care if her mate was male, female, or a blue man from another planet.

She just wanted to find the one person who completed her.

"I'm sorry, Addy. I know Mom and Dad have been pressuring you." Bess turned her big amber eyes back to her.

Addy shrugged. It wasn't as if this was new.

"Seriously, I'm okay. I'm happy for you and Zeff. I'm just being patient," she fibbed.

Bess stared at her, before looking away. Addy hoped her sister didn't pick up on her little white lie.

Addy was trying not to get down. It wouldn't do her any good to burst out crying while they should be enjoying themselves. She loved her siblings and her nephew fiercely and she couldn't wait for her turn to start having pups.

"Well, don't stress over it." Bess stood from her seat and smoothed down her skirt.

Guess she had read through Addy's lie.

"Where are you going?" Addy sat forward.

"I'm going to get me some more punch."

"Here, I'll go—"

"No, I'll get it. I'm not a complete invalid yet." She laughed. She scooped up her empty glass and disappeared into the crowd.

Addy eyed the dancers and chuckled. Most of them could barely stay on the beat. If she were out there, that would be her.

"Okay, Addy girl. We are going to do this," she muttered.

She turned her head at the sound of her name being called. Two guys she had gone to high school with were walking past. Peter and Mario were best friends and known to be troublemakers. They were always the life of any party anywhere they went.

"Hey, guys!" She waved to them, watching them head to the bar.

Anything, girl? she asked her wolf.

Her wolf whined but didn't even lift her head.

Just great.

Nothing.

She had the entire summer to look for her mate. Addy was a third-grade teacher for the Howling Valley elementary school and loved her job. Normally, she spent the summers having fun, but this year was going be focused on her.

Maybe she needed to broaden her search.

There were a few towns located near her where she could go visit. Determination filled her.

She was going to go hunt for her mate.

* * *

"So what are you planning to do? Just go around to different towns sniffing everyone?" Malissa cackled as if she had just told the funniest joke ever.

Addy glared at her best friend.

Seriously?

Sniff people?

"This isn't funny," Addy grumbled. Her wolf had more common sense than that.

She'd just wait for the breeze to carry their scent to her.

It was a beautiful day outside, and the two of them were lying out in Addy's yard soaking up the sun. She couldn't think of a better way to spend a lazy day then nude sunbathing, and drinking ice-cold lemonade to relax. The warmth of the sun kissed her bare skin.

Malissa was a gorgeous girl, blonde hair, hazel eyes, and a curvy body that always snagged the attention of anyone with a pulse who was in her presence. They had been best friends since they were pups. Addy's gaze ran over her friend, testing her wolf's response.

Nothing.

The fact that both of them were naked didn't bother either of them. Shifters were used to it. Shifting from a human form to animal, the clothes never survived.

Addy rested her chin on her forearms and stared off at the woods behind her home. She enjoyed these types of days. Teaching third grade children was very stressful and time-consuming. Dealing with rambunctious children all day was exhausting yet rewarding.

The summer break was her time to unwind.

"Don't take that tone of voice with me, young lady." Malissa chuckled. "I'm just trying to find the humor in this."

"You aren't feeling any longing to find your mate?" Addy asked quietly.

Malissa grew silent. She played with the grass in front of her before responding.

"I guess. I mean, I'm having fun being single, but it would be nice to come home to someone who loves me unconditionally, share a link with someone where I know I will always be able to count on them, and not be alone as I grow old."

They fell into a comfortable silence. Addy closed her eyes and focused on the warmth caressing her body. She tried to block out all thoughts of searching for her mate, but she couldn't. It was overwhelming her, so she knew her wolf had to be feeling it, too.

"Well, if you must know, Grove Hill will be hosting a pack run, and they are inviting shifters from all over to participate. It's a social event, and I was thinking of going," Addy said softly. A smile played on her lips. "And no, I don't plan on walking up to everyone and sniffing them."

"If you want, I'll go with you."

Addy opened her eyes and turned to her friend. Malissa had her infamous grin in place.

"I'm sure we will have fun."

"We will. Even if we don't find our mates, we can find something to occupy our time." Malissa winked. Her friend was always the center of attention wherever they went. In college, she'd dragged Addy to all of the hottest parties and ensured she'd had a good time.

Addy snorted, shaking her head.

"What? They have some available wolves over there that are drool-worthy."

Grove Hill was located about an hour away from Howling Valley. It was another small town that was friendly to all paranormals. She knew a few people who lived there, and it would be a fun trip.

"We'll see. Not sure if I just want to hook up with just anyone." Addy rolled her eyes.

Shifters had healthy sexual appetites and great stamina when it came to sex. Memories of her last relationships came to mind. Addy wasn't ashamed of her past. She'd had male and female lovers. Even now, if she wanted to scratch an itch, there were a few she could call and they would be over immediately.

But that wasn't what she was focused on. She could find good sex anywhere, but she wanted more.

"Don't count anything out now. You never know who you will meet." Malissa shrugged. Her friend gave her that familiar look that she didn't believe Addy would keep an open mind.

"Okay. If I think someone is hot, I'll go for it. Mating call or no."

"That's my girl." Malissa chuckled. "We need to take this time and live life to the fullest. We are young and free."

Malissa rested her head on her folded arms. Addy stared at her for a moment, not responding.

Young and free.

Having fun.

She smiled sadly at her friend who clearly didn't understand what she was experiencing. Maybe it was just the call to mate hadn't hit Malissa yet. Addy was older than her by a few months.

Her animal whined, sitting up from where she lay.

What is it? she asked.

Her beast snorted and didn't say another word.

Just great.

Her damn animal was going to drive her crazy with her nonchalant attitude.

Addy just prayed that whenever she did come into the presence of her mate, her animal would act a little interested.

Chapter Two

Howling Valley.

Cora Latimer stood at the edge of the woods and stared at the welcome sign to the town. Hope filled her that this would be her last stop and she would be safe here.

She opened herself up and sensed the other paranormals living in the area. She breathed a sigh of relief. She'd heard it was a paranormal-friendly town, but she was going to have to keep a low profile. She had traveled a long way and was ready to stay in one place for a while.

Her feet carried her into town.

Hefting the straps of her bag onto her shoulder, she tipped her chin up. She was going to make a fresh start here. At twenty-five years old, she was ready to start living her life.

Good things were bound to come from Howling Valley.

Deep down, she felt it all the way to her bones.

For some reason, she was drawn to this little hidden gem. Unsure why, but a week ago she was reviewing a map of Southern California, and her gaze had landed on the name Howling Valley. The way her body had reacted to the name, she'd known she had to come.

The goddess above would lead her to her destiny.

Cora had put all of her faith in the goddess to lead her where she was supposed to be.

She'd researched the town, and when she saw it proclaimed it was friendly to paranormals, she knew it was to be her next move.

It was far enough away from home that no one should be able to find her. She'd taken precautions of covering her tracks. If anyone was trying to search for her, they would follow her leads that would suggest she'd gone east.

She'd arrived in Howling Valley last night and had set up camp deep in the woods on the outskirts of town. All of her personal belongs she was able to take with her were hidden away.

She was one with nature.

A witch who was grounded to Mother Earth.

She had set up and hidden herself behind a ward. Forest animals strolled past her, sensing something odd, but weren't able to see her or walk through her barriers she'd created.

It was her safe haven and the only way she'd be able to sleep at night.

As she drew closer to town, she pulled back on her powers, disguising herself. She wanted to check the townspeople out first before relaxing. She was sure there had to be a coven here. Eventually she would have to touch base with the leader if she were to remain.

Not that she had any plans of joining one.

A bitter taste entered her mouth at the thought of her former coven.

If word that a powerful witch appeared out of nowhere, word might make its way back home.

She couldn't afford that.

Not after she'd fought so hard to escape.

It just about broke her to leave, but it was what was best.

For everyone.

Dragging in a trembling breath, she pushed the thoughts of her past away. She didn't have a home yet, but she was determined to find one.

She was in search of somewhere she could claim, and hopefully Howling Valley was it.

Glancing down at herself, she had dressed as presentable as one could living in the wild. Her long navy skirt flowed around her ankles, her peasant white shirt was crisp and light. She'd brushed her dark midnight hair until it practically shined.

What she wouldn't give for a warm bath. She planned to search for housing. As much as she loved nature, a girl would kill for hot running water and a soft mattress to sleep on.

In her travels, she'd occasionally rented a hotel room, paying cash only.

Thankfully with her powers, she could alter people's memories of her to not leave any trace of her behind once she left.

She was tired of living out of her tent. It was time for her to find somewhere to call home. She was glad her parents had instilled in her skills to live off the land. It had certainly come in handy.

Dallan and Lavender Latimer were loving parents who'd helped her escape the clutches of their coven high priest.

She could remember the last time she'd seen her parents. Her father had distracted the coven who were hunting her down while her mother helped her out of town. Tears blurred her vision. She blinked them back. She had to remain strong. Her parents had risked so much to help their only daughter run. It pained her that she didn't know what had happened to them.

Were they captured?

Punished?

It was too dangerous for her to reach out to them to find out.

She dared not think of her brother, Marden.

He had sided with the coven.

Even though it had been months since that night, the betrayal was still fresh and ran deep.

Her only brother had betrayed her and their family.

Cora arrived in town. She strolled along the sidewalk, keeping her head down. She didn't want to draw any unwanted attention. She scanned the area, looking at the storefronts.

The aroma of deliciousness hit her. Her stomach chose that moment to growl. She was hungry. She had been living off rations she'd collected and saved. She had a stash of money saved up that she had budgeted off of. She had done well, but eventually she would need to find a way to make a living.

Today, she could splurge on a good hot meal.

That was her one reward when she arrived at new towns. Trying to remain off the radar, she stayed away from major cities and their technologies, but instead stuck to slow back towns where they were behind the modern world.

Cora was from Oceana, Washington, a small town located directly on the Pacific Ocean. Her previous coven may be locked in a remote area, but they had reach. The high priest—

She cut her train of thought.

No more thinking of them.

Lifting her chin, she glanced around and found where the smell was coming from.

Tina's Diner.

Her stomach rumbled again.

"Okay," she muttered. She stopped in front of the restaurant and hesitated for two seconds before grasping the door and opening it. She stepped inside, and immediately, her mouth watered.

Yup, this was the right place.

The decor reminded her of an early nineteenth-century diner, with large tables, stools, and vinyl booths that could fit an entire army. Her attention landed on a board on the wall of the waiting area. She ambled over to it.

There were advertisements for piano lessons, electronics for sale, an upcoming country fair, automobile sales. Her gaze stopped on a piece of paper for an apartment for rent.

That piqued her interest.

Over the garage. Loft apartment with a small kitchen, bath, fully furnished and private entrance. Available now.

The price was in her range.

She tore off a serrated end that held the phone number to call.

"Hello, dear. Can we help you?" a cheerful voice offered behind her.

Cora spun around on her heel and greeted the woman with a smile. She tucked the tiny piece of paper in her purse so she could call them later.

"Yes, table for one, please," Cora said.

"Sure, dear." She was a plump woman with her hair drawn back in a tight bun. Her tag displayed her name of Barb. She grabbed a menu and utensils and waved for Cora to follow her. "Here you go."

Barb motioned to a booth near the windows.

Cora stiffened at first, not wanting to be put on display, but she didn't want to appear odd.

"Thank you." She took her seat and placed her purse on her lap.

"You're welcome." Barb sat the menu and utensils on the table in front of her. "You must be new to town."

"Oh, what gave me away?" Cora raised an eyebrow. Obviously, the woman was very observant. Cora glanced around the restaurant, taking in humans and shifters.

"A pretty thing like yourself, I would remember." Barb laughed. She rested a hand on her plump hip and shook her head. "But seriously, hun, this is a small town, and we practically all know each other."

"Oh." Cora smiled, trying to appear friendly.

"But don't worry, we welcome strangers for whatever reasons they blow into town."

"Thank you."

"Can I get you something to drink? Your server will be over shortly."

Cora scanned the menu and decided on a Coke. Barb gave her a smile and scurried off.

Cora relaxed back against the booth. She picked up the menu and studied it. Everything on there made her stomach rumble. She eyed the prices and figured she could splurge even more.

Barb brought back her Coke just as her waitress, Lara, came over. Cora found herself smiling at the funny banter between the women. She could easily see the two were friends. Lara and Barb made her feel welcome.

"I'll be back with your order soon. The kitchen isn't busy now. You just beat the lunch rush," Lara said. She gave Cora a wide grin before walking away.

Cora turned to the window and decided to people-watch. There were quite a few people milling round. The town was livelier than she initially thought it would be, but then again, she'd arrived yesterday and hadn't really ventured out.

But now seeing it late morning, townsfolk were out and about strolling along the sidewalks. Traffic was light on the streets, and Cora got a sense of a cozy community.

A few people looked at her through the window, offered a smile and a nod. She relaxed even more.

This was the right choice.

She was sure of it.

"Here you go, darling. Let me know if you need anything else." Lara arrived with her plate.

Cora's mouth watered at the sight of her fried chicken special. It had sounded good on the menu and looked even better on the plate.

"Thank you."

Lara gave a wave and moved on to another table where Barb had just seated them.

Cora took her time eating her meal. It had been at least a week since she'd had a hot one. So she wanted to cherish it. The rations she had back in her tent were for survival and didn't taste anywhere as good as what was sitting in front of her.

Once she finished her meal, she pulled out cash and left a tip for Lara then made her way up to the register.

"How was your food?" Barb asked, ringing her up.

"Delicious." Cora smiled and handed Barb exact change for the meal.

"Well, I hope while you are in town that you come back and visit us."

"Most definitely. I will." Cora peered around and saw a phone on the wall near Barb. "By chance, can I make a quick call?"

She didn't have cell phone. She couldn't risk being tracked by it, so hers had been left when she'd run. It was for the best.

"Sure, honey." Barb waved her over to it.

Cora moved behind the counter and pulled the little slip of paper from her purse. She picked up the phone and rested it on her shoulder while she dialed the number. A few minutes later, she hung up with an offer for her to go see the apartment.

Yes, the goddess was watching out for her.

"Rent is due at the first of the month," Chuck said. The owner of the house was human, a slightly portly man who had shared with her that his son used to live above the garage before he'd moved to Houston. "All utilities are included. Washer and dryer is down in the garage."

Cora glanced around the room and had to beat her excitement down. The apartment was more than she had hoped for.

Chuck lived near the edge of town. His land backed up to parts of the woods that surrounded Howling Valley. She couldn't ask for a better location. The garage was detached and positioned behind the house, allowing her to have all the privacy she needed. An entrance to the apartment was situated on the side of the structure, and she didn't have to go through his garage to get up to her loft.

The place was cozy, with a designated living area, a small kitchenette, and a bathroom. There was a Murphy bed along the wall.

It was everything she needed.

"It's really nice," she murmured. She turned back to face him to find him studying her.

"You aren't one of them shifters, are you?" he asked, tilting his head to the side.

"No," she replied quickly. That was a weird question, considering he lived in a shifter town.

"I just don't want to chance a shifter coming in here and tearing this place up. I once rented it to a young man, one of those wolves, and he practically destroy it. Took me a while to make it livable again."

Cora shrugged. It sort of made sense, but she hoped he wasn't prejudiced to paranormals. She wouldn't share with him what she was. To his human eye, she appeared to be like him.

But to a paranormal, once she let her guard down, they would know without a doubt what she was.

"You won't have any issues from me."

"Where'd you say you were from?" He

scratched his head.

"Portland," the lie rolled off her tongue. She'd had plenty of time to think of her background story she would share with people in order to protect her identity.

An only child, parents deceased and from Portland. Her gypsy life was due to her not having attachments and wanting to discover this big, beautiful country.

The story worked every time someone asked.

"Well, the place is yours if you want it." He gave her a nod, appearing satisfied with everything she had shared with him.

"Thank you. I really appreciate it." She glanced around once more with a sense of relief filling her.

She would have a nice bed to sleep in and still be close to nature.

It was the best of both worlds.

Chapter Three

Her four legs carried her as fast as they could go. The need to stretch out her legs had taken over her. Addy raced along the familiar area of land.

Small animals hid in the presence of a hunter. Her wolf grinned, loving the freedom she was given.

In her wolf form, Addy was still in control. She was in the background while her wolf got to be herself. Between the two, Addy was still the dominant. Her wolf may not like all of her choices, but she went along with them.

Addy had been born and raised in Howling Valley, and she loved her town. Twenty-nine years, and she had yet to tire of this beautiful settlement.

It was picturesque and still held on to the old charm from the past.

The beautiful lands of the compound were something all wolves prided themselves on. The area was lush, supple, and just majestic.

The one thing that sat in the back of her mind was if she did find a mate from another town, where would they live? She would certainly miss Howling Valley.

Her wolf snorted.

I know, I could always come back to visit. Addy rolled her eyes. She was sure once she found her special someone, they could have an adult conversation about where they would live.

She slowed to a trot and breathed in the enticing aroma of a bed of flowers near her. She scampered over to them, wanting to inhale more of their scent.

She and her wolf needed this.

Leaning over the wildflowers, she drew in a breath, appreciating her special find. She glanced around and took in the amazing area. Tall trees, bright-green lands, bushes, and wide, open blue skies greeted her.

Her wolf wanted to roam, and that was what Addy was letting her do.

A rustling in the brush close by snagged her attention. Addy curiously crept forward to see what was making the noise.

Her wolf was already anticipating a chase. Addy sat in the background and handed the reins over to her wolf. If she wanted to chase rabbits or squirrels, so be it.

Her gaze connected with a rabbit that immediately turned and sped off.

Addy was right behind it.

Her wolf loved the thrill of a good chase. She sped after the animal, going deeper into the thick foliage.

Addy slowed down, having lost sight of the rabbit. Her wolf whined, disappointed she hadn't caught it. Her breaths were coming fast, her heart pounding.

Addy paused, her ears picking up a different sound.

Was that someone cursing?

She turned in the direction of the voice and held still. She strained to hear exactly where it was coming form. As far she was in the forest, there shouldn't be anyone out this way. She lifted her nose and inhaled, trying to catch a scent.

"Dammit," a soft voice snapped.

Quietly, she crept forward and peered through a dense row of bushes. Her wolf sensed someone was near, but her eyes must have been playing tricks on her.

There was nothing there.

She sniffed the air, inhaling a sweet honeysuckle scent.

Honeysuckle didn't grow in these parts.

Her wolf perked up while her heart raced. A low growl escaped her.

Mate.

Addy was completely confused. Was her wolf losing it?

She stepped back, unsure of where the sound and smell were coming from. Had she became so consumed with finding a mate that she was starting to imagine voices and aromas?

"For the love of all that is holy."

Addy froze. The hair on the back of her animal's neck rose. The pounding of her pulse in her ears drowned out everything around her.

She could only hear that beautiful, melodious voice.

Her. Mate.

Addy closed her eyes and absorbed it. If she heard it again, she would recognize it anywhere. A shiver went down her spine at the huskiness and the attitude. It was sexy and held a distinct notion that whoever it belonged to would have fire in her.

Addy wouldn't want a docile mate. She was a shifter and would want someone to challenge her, be an equal to her, and would stroke the flames of passion that would surely be between them.

Adrenaline raced through her system. She pushed forward carefully, scanning the area.

She blinked, and out of thin air appeared an entire campground. Her gaze landed on the lone figure struggling with a tent.

A witch.

A powerful one who could put up wards of invisibility to stay hidden.

And she was absolutely the most gorgeous woman Addy had ever seen. Her knees grew temporarily weak.

Finally.

Addy had put all of her faith into the fates, and now she was being rewarded.

She knew it.

If she just waited, the right person would be put in her path.

The woman's long flowing hair was almost midnight in color. She was dressed in leggings and a tunic that stopped just beneath the roundness of her ass. Her outfit did little to hide the curvy womanly figure. Addy took in her shapely legs and full breasts.

Mate, her wolf growled again.

Need and desire for her almost brought Addy to her knees. Her body tensed with the sole purpose of claiming the woman. She wanted to memorize the delicious scent. Strip her of all of her clothing and dive face-first in between her thighs so she could taste all of her.

Addy salivated at the thought of licking her mate to orgasm.

Addy watched the woman finally get the tent to collapse. She scurried around as if packing up.

Why would she need to be hidden?

Why was she sleeping in the woods when there were two good hotels in town?

And who the hell was she?

Addy remained as still as she could, not wanting to alert the witch to her presence.

She had yet to see the woman's eyes, and already the intense desire to sink her fangs into her flawless skin was consuming her.

She had to get closer to her.

Finally, the woman appeared to be finished packing up her belongings.

A stark fear overtook Addy.

The witch couldn't leave.

The beauty tossed her heavy bag onto her back and grabbed another one in her hand. She glanced around as if checking to ensure she hadn't forgotten anything. She turned and headed in the opposite direction of Addy, disappearing into the woods.

Addy's heart just about jumped out of her chest.

She had to follow her.

Addy remained back, away from the witch. If she were to get any closer, she feared she'd lose control of her beast. It was taking everything in her power to keep her animal for racing forward to the woman.

That was not how she imagined them meeting for the first time. Addy devised a plan. Find out where she was going, then go home, shift to her human form, put on clothes, then race back so she could go and speak with her.

It wouldn't be until they were mated that they

could share an intense connection between them where they would be able to sense the other's emotions, thoughts, and possibly communicate with each other.

Addy had heard of mates sharing a bond that no one else could create. The craving to have one's mate would never go away but enhance tenfold.

Addy couldn't even begin to fathom what that would mean.

At the moment she was downwind from her mate, and that sweet honeysuckle scent she wore was driving Addy crazy. She inhaled it, and it rocked her to her core.

She may be in her wolf form, but it was still painfully arousing.

Her clit pulsated with need.

Maybe it was good she was in her wolf form.

Addy's body was throbbing with an intense awakening that only her mate would be able to satisfy.

It was safe to be in animal form. She wouldn't be able to act on the urges. Addy tried to block all of the fantasies of what she wanted to do to the witch from her mind, but it was getting harder the more she inhaled her scent.

With her sensitive wolf nose, she could pick up

thousands of smells, but the only one filling her senses was the one of her mate.

Addy became aware of the silence in the air. There were no other animals present. She cursed internally. Certainly, the witch would have picked up on it.

A quiet forest would alert anyone that a predator must be near.

Addy paused, listening for the footsteps of her mate.

She didn't hear anything. Had the witch figured out she was being followed? Addy crept forward along the path before hopping into the brush.

Quiet footsteps made their way toward her.

She peeked through the leaves of the bushes, keeping her body low to the ground.

The witch appeared, looking around. Her dark hair floated through the air as she spun in a circle, scanning the area.

Yup, she had picked up on Addy's presence.

"Hello?" the witch called out.

Addy closed her eyes, basking in the sound of her voice. A shiver rocked her as desire roared in her body.

She had to claim this woman.

Chapter Four

Someone or something was following her.

Of that, Cora was certain.

Her heart rate was racing, and her skin grew warm. Awareness prickled on her skin. Someone was watching her.

She glanced around, but she didn't see anyone.

"Maybe I'm going crazy." Being on the run for so long was finally catching up to her.

That had to be it.

Cora closed her eyes and inhaled sharply. She didn't know why her body was trembling the way it was. She tried to get her breathing under control.

Small waves of desire flickered inside her.

"What is going on?" she whispered. Her body

was behaving out of the norm. There was no reason she should be feeling this way.

Cora would have to admit it had been a while since she'd had sex with another person. Since she'd been on the run, it had been her and her trusty finger.

There hadn't been any time to grab her B.O.B.

What a shame.

Blowing out a deep breath, she opened her eyes and tried to fight the urge.

She turned around and made her way back to where she had dropped her belongings. She would get to her new home, take a nice long shower, scratch her itch that was suddenly making itself known, then go to sleep. It would feel so good to finally lie in a real bed for more than a day.

Her body was aching and tired of lying on the hard ground. Her sleeping bag just didn't cut it. She could still feel all of the rocks and bumps underneath the tent.

Hefting up her large duffle bag, she slid her arms through the loops so it would rest on her back while picking up her other one and carrying it in her hand.

It shouldn't take her much longer to get to her apartment.

Excitement filled her that she would finally have a place to call her own. Confident everything would work out, she made the trek to her new apartment.

Now that she had a town she would be calling home, she would be able to finally relax and live her life. She knew she would always have to watch her back and maintain the story she had concocted, but the little white lies would be worth it.

For her safety and anyone she developed a relationship with.

That was one thing she missed.

Being on the run didn't allow her to get close to anyone. She had met some people on her journey, but she had to keep them at arm's length.

What she wouldn't give to be able to settle down with her soul mate, create a warm and loving home, and raise children.

Witches were born with a 'knowing' inside them. When their other half presented to them, they just knew. There was no way to explain it. The moon goddess overhead chose who was to be their other half.

The goddess was never wrong.

Only the moon goddess knew exactly who the perfect soul mate was for her. Cora had been taught that from the time she was old enough to understand what a soul mate was.

Dallan and Lavender Latimer were soul mates, and it was rare for them to just find each other in the same town. She was a lucky girl, being able to see how much they were in love with each other.

It was a beautiful thing to see. Her parents shared a bond so close. Cora prayed the goddess would bless her the way she had blessed them.

As a young witch going through puberty, she had not only the birds and bees chat with her mother, but that of the knowing.

"Momma, but how did you know Daddy was the one?" A wide-eyed Cora had glanced up at her mother.

Lavender had reached out and taken Cora's hand in hers. They were as close as mother and daughter could be. She patted Cora's hand and smiled.

"There's no way to explain, but you will have no doubt in your mind when it's your turn. All it took was one look into your father's eyes, and I was a goner."

Cora blew out a deep breath. She couldn't wait for that moment, but for now, she had to worry about surviving.

A shiver passed through her. Derwin Cross, the high priest of her coven, Oasis Moon, was gunning for her. After their former priestess had died, Derwin had taken over with his reign, turning the coven dark.

It had always been rumored that Derwin was involved in the darkest of magic, but no one dared say anything. Brumelda, his predecessor, had believed he would be her rightful heir. He, the nephew of the former leader of the coven, was chosen after her untimely death.

Once he had control over the Oasis Moon, everything changed.

Derwin had set his sights on her. He wanted her. His greed for power led him to pursue her. He wanted to harness her magic and use it for the dark.

Cora's powers had been no secret, but she still respected her elders and her former priestess who had helped train her to use what the goddess had blessed her with.

Cora would never turn dark. She was meant for the light.

Derwin, unable to take no for an answer, had issued an order for her capture.

She had almost not escaped.

Her brother, Marden, had joined Derwin and had ratted out the plans of her escape.

Marden had fallen for the evilness and the ideas the new high priest had for the coven. Derwin and the council had gone to war with each other.

He wanted to strip them of their power in the coven and take over as a dictator of sorts. The coven had been divided.

Marden had sided with Derwin, and for that, she would never forgive him. She didn't know what she would do if she ever saw him again. She just hoped he had not harmed their parents.

She prayed to the goddess above that her parents were able to escape. She hated they had sacrificed themselves for her.

The hairs on her arms rose suddenly, along with the appearance of goosebumps.

Whoever had been following her was back.

She paused and glanced behind her, finding the path empty.

Her nipples grew painfully taut into buds, while her body suddenly became hypersensitive.

Goddess above, what was happening to her?

Her breaths came fast, her pulse pounded, and her body became sexually aware of whoever was near her.

It was time to end this.

Whoever this was needed to present themselves.

Now.

Cora tore her bags off her and tossed them aside.

"Who is there?" she demanded.

She hated how her voice came out husky. Energy surged through her body to her fingertips in preparation to fight whoever was lurking in the woods.

A growl sounded.

Something came bounding through the woods, this time not bothering to hide their footsteps.

Cora braced herself, her gaze sweeping the area. She spun around, unsure of which direction the animal was coming from.

Wrong move.

She whipped around just in time for a heavy, fur-covered body to slam into hers.

Cora landed with a thud, her eyes squeezing tight as the firm, hard ground caught her. The heated breath of the animal resting on top of her blew in her face.

She waited for the bite that never came.

Cora opened her eyes to find an auburn wolf with amber eyes lying on top of her.

If she didn't know any better, the animal was

grinning.

"What the—?"

She was interrupted by a wide tongue swiping her face in one long lick. The beast snorted, pushing its face into the crook of her neck.

Cora didn't know what to do. She remained still, not wanting the beast to have a sudden change of heart.

Well, at least the beast was extremely friendly.

She closed her eyes again, waiting for the animal to get off her. Hopefully, it would move on. It was probably a teenage shifter completing a dare or something. Back home, witches and warlocks in the teenage years were always known to issue challenges to each other to prove their powers.

Suddenly, the air grew warm, and the shimmer of magic filled the air. Within moments, a warm curvy body molded to her.

Cora gasped.

She opened her eyes to find a beautiful redheaded woman with fiery amber eyes braced above her. Cora's gazed roamed her perfect face, her nose, small and petite, with plump, kissable lips. Her fangs were still descended, peeking from beneath her top lip.

She was naked, her full breasts pressing against

Cora's. The heat from her core was radiating as the lower half of her body straddled Cora's.

The air was ripped from Cora's body. Her body grew painfully aroused as the knowing roared to life inside her.

Oh, goddess above.

It was just as her mother had said.

She would know.

This woman, a wolf shifter, was the other half of her soul.

The woman leaned down again and nuzzled Cora's neck. She breathed in, as if needing to inhale all of Cora's scent.

Cora was completely turned on. Her pussy grew slick with desire. Cora's body shook with the need to be claimed while her breasts were painfully pushing at her bra.

Red lifted and gazed down at Cora again, then lowered her head. Her chest rumbled with a growl just as she pressed her lips to Cora's.

A gasp escaped her lips, and the woman slipped her tongue inside her mouth, stroking her tongue with hers.

Cora could not fight the knowing.

She had never been one to be a prude. She'd had many sexual partners, but none had rendered a reaction like this from her. The kiss deepened. The woman's fingers threaded their way into Cora's hair to hold her in place.

Her knowing urged her to strip off her clothes and allow this shifter to claim her. Her hips rotated, pressing against this naked woman.

She attempted to push her away, but her hand captured a full, soft breast. A moan vibrated from Red. She nipped Cora's lip with her fang.

Cora couldn't help but massage the firm mound, a groan slipping from her.

What am I doing?

Cora blinked.

Hell, she didn't even know the woman's name.

It took all of her strength to tear her mouth from Red's. Their breathing was labored, and they stared at each other.

"You are more beautiful than I could have hoped for," Red whispered. She reached up and trailed a finger along Cora's cheek. Her nostrils flared out slightly. Her amber eyes narrowed on Cora. "You are ready for your woman."

"What?" Cora stuttered. She blinked a few

times, not understanding what the woman was saying.

Red's lips were swollen from their kiss. She smirked, her eyes darkening. She pushed up, hovering over Cora.

"I can scent your wetness." Red licked her lips. Her chest rumbled again; her beast obviously was close to the surface. "You want me to lick your pussy?"

Cora swallowed hard. Images of Red's head between her legs came rushing to her. She let loose a moan.

"No," she said softly, shaking her head.

"No?" Red's eyebrows rose high in disbelief. "But you are aroused. I can smell how wet you are. Let me take care of you."

Red slid down her body and reached for Cora's leggings.

"Wait." Cora held up her hands.

Red paused, her amber eyes watching her. She slid away from her.

Cora crawled in reverse from the woman until she hit a tree. She had to put some distance between them.

Cora couldn't think with the woman touching her.

"What is the matter?" Red asked, her head tilted to the side.

Cora inhaled sharply, taking in the woman's naked body as she knelt on the ground. Her breasts were full with dusty-rose areolas, and her body was toned as a shifter was known to be. Cora's eyes dropped lower, discovering that the carpet matched the drapes on the woman.

"When you look at me like that, I know you are lying about wanting me to put my mouth on you." Red smirked. "I'm a shifter and I can also sense a lie."

"Really? How?" Cora knew she shouldn't be challenging this woman, but dammit, she couldn't help it.

"The pulse at the base of your neck is racing. It skipped a beat the second you said no. It was a lie."

"No, it wasn't a lie. My heart is racing because of what just happened right there." Cora pointed to the spot she had landed during the fall.

Her body was practically on fire.

"What do you want me to do?" Red snagged her bottom lip and chewed on it.

Cora had to tear her eyes away from the sight. She wanted to do nothing but go back to the woman and kiss her again.

"Well, first off, you can start by telling me your name." Cora cleared her throat.

Red's cheeks darkened slightly, and a grin took over her face.

"My name is Adelina Ransome, but all of my friends and family call me Addy." She tucked her dark-ginger hair behind an ear. "What is yours?"

"Cora Latimer, and I'm just called Cora."

"That's a beautiful name." Addy narrowed her eyes on Cora again.

She crawled over to Cora, and it was something about the sight of this woman in this position that drove Cora insane.

"Now that we have the introductions out of the way, I was about to do something we both would like."

"But we just met," Cora blurted out. The intensity of this connection was quite frightening. It wasn't every day a girl had her *knowing* come to life.

Addy stopped near her, the heat of her body washing over Cora. She reached out and cupped Cora's face.

"You feel what is between us, don't you, witch?"

Cora swallowed, jerking her head in a nod. It was no surprise Addy would sense she was a witch.

Her soul mate would recognize her for what she was.

"So why are you resisting? Do witches not instantly act on the mating call?" Addy's gentle caresses sent a shiver of arousal through her body.

Would this ever go away?

Cora was primed and ready for a good, hard fucking, but for some reason she held back.

Maybe it was the fact she was being hunted.

If she were to move on the mating connection, she would want to tell Addy everything up front.

That she was being hunted down, and if Derwin found her, then he would rain hell on their shifter town.

Maybe coming to Howling Valley was a bad idea.

But something had drawn her to this town, and now she knew why. It was the goddess above trying to show her where her other half was.

"We do, but we at least get to know the person first." Cora offered her a tiny smile.

"But we already know the most important thing right know." Addy drew closer to her. Their thighs brushed each other as Addy settled next to her on the ground.

"I know," Cora whispered. She didn't have to

ask what that was. She already knew. Even though they were different species, it would appear their bodies knew they belonged together.

"Your scent is divine. It's driving me crazy." Addy closed her eyes for a brief moment then opened them again. "If we are to do this your way, I only ask one thing."

Her words ended on a growl.

That animalistic nature made Cora's core pulse. She was sure her panties were soaked and wouldn't be surprised if her leggings were, too. Everything about Addy turned Cora on.

It would be hard to deny her anything.

"What is it?"

Addy's hand came to rest on the edge of Cora's leggings. She paused, her eyes already asking for permission.

"Can I have one taste?"

Cora moaned, her body shaking from the desire that was rippling through her body.

She nodded.

Addy's small hand slipped underneath her leggings and panties. Cora widened her thighs to give her better access to her dripping pussy.

Addy's fingers made their way to Cora's slit. She

dipped it into the wetness that had gathered. Addy's chest rumbled her pleasure.

Cora's head fell back against the tree as Cora's finger skated along her clit. She was starting to have doubts about her decision.

It wouldn't hurt for them to fuck first then get to know each other.

Addy's finger played with her nub for a moment before sliding inside her slick channel. A curse escaped Addy's lips.

Cora already knew why.

Her pussy was so damn wet that a river was probably pouring from her.

"You're so fucking wet," Ady murmured. She nuzzled her face into the crook of Cora's neck. Addy pressed hot kisses along her skin and slowly finger-fucked Cora.

Cora shivered at the sensation of sharp fangs.

Just as soon as it began, it was over.

Cora whimpered from the loss of Addy's finger inside her. Addy withdrew her fingers from Cora's pants. Their gazes landed on Addy's fingers coated with her creaminess. Cora sucked in a strangled breath and watched Addy bring those fingers to her lips.

Addy's eyes shut tight, and she licked and sucked her fingers clean.

Cora's core clenched at the sight of pure bliss on Addy's face.

Goddess above.

Maybe waiting wasn't the right idea.

Chapter Five

"You can't travel like that." Cora motioned to Addy's body.

Addy glanced down at herself, only seeing she was naked. She was proud of her body. Her mate grew aroused just by looking at her. The light aroma of her mate's excitement floated through the air.

"What's wrong with me being naked? I'm a shifter." She shrugged. Addy was still trying to get over the fact that her mate was right here next to her. Her plans of taking the entire summer to search could now be cancelled.

She shuddered at the memory of her first taste of Cora.

Her sweat cream was everything. Addy planned

to spend a day with her face buried between Cora's thighs.

A pussy that sweet deserved to be devoured.

"If we are to go to my apartment and my land-lord sees you naked, he would wonder why you have no clothes on." Cora bent down and unzipped one duffle bag. She pulled out another pair of leggings and a t-shirt.

Addy took the clothing. She held the shirt up so she could see the words imprinted on it.

Witches do it better.

She glanced over at Cora who had deep blush spreading along her cheeks.

"I thought it was funny." She chuckled. She closed her bag and stood to her full height.

"I can't wait to test this theory," Addy murmured. She quickly donned the clothing. Not that she a thing against wearing coverings, she just preferred to be in her natural state.

Her wolf was pacing back and forth inside her.

Claim her, her animal snapped.

In due time, she replied. Her gaze landed on Cora who was hefting her bags up on her shoulder.

"Here, I'll take one." Addy reached for the one still on the ground. It was late afternoon, and the sky was a bright blue with the sun shining.

Since she was no longer in her animal form, the sounds of the forest had retuned. It was a beautiful day, and Addy could almost pretend she and Cora were out for a stroll.

But not at the moment. She promised herself that she would take Cora to her favorite spots to share them with her. Excitement filled her that she would be able to spend her life with a beautiful witch.

Addy could sense Cora was very powerful and looked forward to seeing what powers she possessed.

"Thanks," Cora murmured. Her bright-blue eyes were mesmerizing as they met Addy's.

Addy's wolf slammed into her chest. It was impatient, wanting to consummate their mating. She inhaled sharply, the scent of Cora's arousal still lingering in the air.

Addy was trying to beat down her own instincts. Her pussy ached, her breasts were sensitive, and the soft t-shirt brushing against her nipples was pure torture.

Her mate wanted her to have clothes on now, so she wouldn't argue. There was much more she needed to learn about Cora.

"We aren't far from my place." Cora motioned

for her to follow.

Addy moved forward and took Cora's free hand in hers. The need to touch her was strong, and Addy couldn't ignore it, nor did she want to.

"I haven't seen you around. When did you move to Howling Valley?" Addy asked.

"Two nights ago," Cora replied. She glanced over at Addy, and it was apparent she was hiding something.

"Why are you staying in the woods? Why not your place?"

Cora didn't answer at first. Addy was unsure if she was going to. Cora stared straight ahead, the grip of her hand tightening around Addy's.

"It's a long story, and with this thing between us, I plan to tell you the entire truth, but now isn't the right time."

Addy's curiosity was getting the best of her. What was going on? With as much gear as Cora traveled with, it was evident her mate had been living off the land for a while.

From what she knew, witches were bound to the earth, but she didn't think Cora would be living out in the woods unless she was hiding from something or someone.

"Are you in danger?" Addy asked. Her wolf

stood to attention at this question. Her beast issued a low growl in warning. She would defend her mate without question.

Shifters were naturally protective, and Addy was no different than any other wolf she knew.

Cora flicked her gaze to Addy before looking back away. She jerked her head in a nod.

A growl was ripped from Addy's chest. She swung Cora around and brought her flush to her body.

"No one will harm you while there is breath in my lungs," Addy snapped. Her fangs had yet to retreat back into her gums. They hadn't been in each other's presence long, and already her wolf was bonding to Cora.

Cora's eyes widened, and her lips moved, but no words came.

"Do you understand me?" Addy demanded. She needed to hear confirmation that her mate trusted she could keep her safe. Addy was willing to do what she needed to prove it.

"Yes, but—"

"I meant what I said." Addy leaned forward, dropping a kiss on Cora's lips. Her wolf paced back and forth, on edge. Not one hair would be harmed on Cora's head.

"I...I believe you," Cora whispered.

Satisfied, Addy strode forward, towing Cora behind her.

"Come. We must go to your place so we may speak in private."

"Well, shouldn't I be the one leading since I know where I live?" Cora gave a nervous chuckle.

"Once we get to the edge of the woods then you can take over." Addy glanced back over her shoulder. She tried to smile, to lighten the air. She knew these woods like the back of her hand.

Cora brought herself next to Addy. They walked along in a comfortable silence.

"Tell me about yourself," Cora said.

Addy scented her nervousness. Her mate should not be nervous around her. Addy tried to soften her features. She realized she was being an overbearing shifter, but she couldn't help it.

Her mate was beautiful, powerful, and the sweet aroma of her arousal still lingered in the air.

Relax, girl.

Her wolf snorted, constantly on alert.

"What do you want to know?" Addy countered.

"Have you always lived in Howling Valley?" Cora asked. Their stride slowed, with Cora moving closer to her.

Addy liked the fact that Cora felt comfortable to lean into her. She didn't know much about witches, but if getting to know a person first before mating was common amongst them, then Addy would do it.

Most shifters mated first then got to know each other. They allowed their animal instinct to take over.

Bess had met her mate, Nolan, and they had claimed each other the same night. Her sister had been gone for days. The last sighting of her had been leaving a pack function with the tall wolf.

They all figured it was the call to mate.

Bess had returned home happily mated.

Her brother, Zeff, basically the same story when he had met Lynn. They had met at a mutual friend's party and hadn't separated since.

Addy was willing to learn patience.

"Yes, born and raised. My pack started this town," she said proudly. She hefted the strap of Cora's bag higher on her shoulder. "My alpha's family settled here and started the Nightstar Pack."

"I had heard this town was home to paranormals and humans. Does everyone truly get along?"

"Just about. We are no different than any other

community. You have your good citizens and then the ones you have to keep an eye on."

"Hmm…" They grew quiet walking along the trail. They were almost to the edge and soon would no longer have the cover of the woods. "So, what do you do in Howling Valley?"

Addy grinned. As much as she always looked forward to the summers, she had to admit she loved her job.

"I teach third grade at the elementary school."

"Really?" Cora gasped.

"What?" Addy eyed Cora who burst out laughing.

"Nothing. You just don't look like any third grade teach I had back in the day." Cora snorted.

Addy found herself smiling along with her mate.

"Well, I am, and I love what I do." She couldn't help but ask a question of her own. "What did you do for a living before you came here?"

Cora stiffened for a moment. Addy was uncertain if she would answer. Cora glanced at the sky first then blew out a deep breath.

"I was a healer. A master of herbs and was able to use my gifts to help people," she replied softly.

Addy was appreciative of her answering her

question. They broke through the forest and entered a clearing. They were on the outskirts of town. A few homes were nearby that should only take them a few minutes to reach Cora's street.

"Come on. We are close. I shall lead us now."

Cora pushed open the door to her new apartment. After giving Chuck the first month's rent, she had journeyed to the store and bought the food and supplies she would need.

After dropping her items off, she had returned to her campground to break it down.

"The landlord, was he nice to you?" Addy asked, stepping across the threshold.

"Sure. A little weird," Cora admitted. She followed behind Addy and shut the door. She walked over near the couch and sat her bag down. A sigh escaped her from relief of not having to lug the bag anymore.

"Weird? How?" Addy dropped her bag next to Cora's and moved farther into the apartment.

Cora watched how she ambled around. Her movements were that of an animal. If Cora wouldn't have already known, she would have just assumed Addy was some type of predator. Her eyes didn't miss anything.

Cora moved over to the couch and plopped down.

"Well, he outright asked me if I was a shifter." Cora tugged on her sandals and took them off. Her feet were a little sore. She should have put on more sensible shoes with all the walking she had been doing today.

"Hmmm…" Addy grumbled.

"What is that noise for?" Cora leaned back against the pillows. What she wanted to do was take a nice, long hot shower, but that would have to wait for later.

She and Addy had plenty to discuss, and from the looks of Addy, that chat would be today.

"Chuck Grant doesn't like shifters. He's one of the humans who protest about intermingling of the species." Addy turned and stared at her from across the room.

"Then why live in a town that was started by shifters?"

What sense did that make? Not that Cora would condone prejudice against anyone or a species: if one doesn't like them, why move to be around them?

"Who knows." Addy arrived at the refrigerator and peered inside.

"If you are hungry, I can make us something to eat." She was glad that she had gone to the market first.

But if she had gone and cleared her campground first, there was the chance she wouldn't have met Addy.

Goddess, you are one sneaky being.

Cora pushed up off the couch and strolled over to Addy. She leaned against the counter next to her.

The knowing sense inside her roared at their closeness.

Cora's breath caught in her throat. Addy's eyes were practically glowing. She shut the fridge and stood in front of Cora, trapping her in place.

"I didn't pick up much since I was walking, but there's enough for a few days," Cora murmured. Butterflies filled her stomach at their closeness. Addy's eyes were locked on her like a predator who had decided on his prey.

She bit her lip, thinking how bad she wanted to feel Addy's mouth on her. The little preview from the woods was still on her mind.

"I don't want you staying here," Addy

announced. She cupped Cora's cheek softly, running her thumb along Cora's bottom lip.

"Why not?" A nervous laugh escaped Cora.

Addy closed the gap between them. Their breasts pressed against each other.

"I've already paid my rent for the month."

"Did he make you sign a contract?" Addy leaned over and nestled her face into the crook of Cora's neck.

Cora had lost count of the times she had done this. The warmth of Addy's breath caressed her skin. She breathed in deeply as if she were trying to memorize the scent of Cora.

"Well, no. We agreed monthly since I didn't know how long I would be here." A low growl filled the air. That must not have been the right thing to say. "I meant be here. If I found something better, I didn't want to be locked in for an entire year."

Addy planted a hot kiss on her skin, and Cora's control slipped.

Addy trailed kisses up along the column of her neck until their lips merged into a deep, passionate kiss.

Her heart fluttered.

The knowing flared inside her. It was getting harder to resist Addy.

Why must she fight what she knew was meant to be?

Her body flushed with heat as Addy controlled the kiss. Her hands slid along Cora's torso and landed on her ass.

Cora wrapped her arms around Addy, needing to be closer.

They had too many clothes on.

She reached down and grabbed Addy's borrowed shirt and tugged it over head.

Addy's breasts came into view, and it was then Cora caved.

Chapter Six

Addy would take what Cora offered her. Apparently, her mate had had a change of heart. Addy's wolf howled inside at the joy that their mate wanted them.

Cora's heated gaze caressed her skin. Addy stood tall, only a few inches more than Cora, and waited while she took her all in. Addy reached for her leggings and pushed them off.

Cora's quick intake of breath fueled the fire burning bright inside Addy.

"Can I?" Addy asked quietly. She gripped the edge of Cora's top and paused. If her mate were to change her mind, she would back away from her. It would be hard, but she would abide by Cora's wishes.

Cora jerked her head into a nod.

Relief filled Addy. She quickly removed the shirt and froze in place. The black lace bra cupping her breasts was downright sexy, and the sight of Cora's round mounds underneath it was breathtaking.

Addy loved lingerie just like the next girl, but for now it would be better suited on the floor.

"Touch me," Cora whispered.

Addy's gaze flickered to hers before she moved. She grasped Cora by the waist and pulled her back to her. She claimed Cora's lips in a deep kiss, while her hands slid along Cora's soft skin. She carefully removed the offending contraption from Cora without ripping it off.

Cora's hands were busy as well. They skated along Addy's stomach, one headed for her breast while the other went around and molded to her ass.

Mate.

The word fluttered in the back of Addy's head. A growl tore from her as she pushed down Cora's leggings. They broke apart for a mere second so Cora could kick them off.

Addy walked Cora backwards toward the couch. Her animal paced back and forth.

"Your eyes," Cora murmured.

They made it around the edge of the couch until her legs bumped into the front of it.

"What about them?" Addy's words ended on a growl.

"I can see your animal," she replied softly.

Addy cupped the back of Cora's neck. The room was filled with sexual tension, but something was off.

Something was missing.

"Why are you hiding yourself?" Addy asked. She pressed close to Cora, trailing small kisses along her collarbone.

"What are you talking about?" Cora's voice ended on a hitch.

"You are a witch, and I can barely feel your powers." Addy lifted her head and stared into Cora's eyes. "Why are you hiding what you are?"

"I don't know what—"

"Don't lie to me," Addy snarled. There was a growing madness in her. She wanted all of her mate, not some hollow shell.

"Because it would be dangerous if I unleashed all of my powers." Cora's body trembled. Her eyes searched Addy's. She reached up and cupped her cheek. "I promise. I will tell you. Soon."

Addy didn't like the fact that Cora had secrets.

There was a something in her eyes that didn't sit right with Addy.

Was it fear?

Cora leaned forward slightly and nipped Addy's bottom lip.

A growl ripped through Addy. She pushed Cora down onto the couch. She lay sprawled, with her legs wide and her hair wildly displayed on the cushions.

She couldn't take her eyes off her beautiful mate.

No longer able to resist, Addy knelt on the floor before her. Cora's body was everything Addy could wish for. Her eyes were drawn to the center of her mate.

Her pussy was slick and glistening with her juices. She inhaled, breathing in the seductive, intoxicating scent.

Addy eased forward and captured Cora's nipple between her lips.

She suckled hard, eliciting a cry from Cora. Her hands came up and threaded their way into Addy's thick hair. The sight of her dark nipples was driving her crazy. They were just as sweet as they appeared. She took her time bathing the first one before switching over to the other one.

"Yes," Cora cried out. Her grip on Addy's hair tightened.

Once Addy had her fill of Cora's delectable mounds, she decided to move farther down. There was more of Cora that needed to be explored, and she was going to do it right now.

Since taking in the aroma of her woman's desires, all Addy could think about was licking Cora to oblivion.

Cora writhed on the couch with each kiss Addy pressed to her soft belly. She wanted to bring Cora so much pleasure she would not be able to think of any of her past lovers and only want to be with her.

Addy gripped Cora by her ankles and brought her feet to rest on the edge of the couch. Cora's knees dropped to the side, opening herself for Addy.

The scent of Cora's arousal grew thicker. It was consuming Addy. She would forever remember this moment. Cora spread-eagled, exposing her pink pussy just for her.

Her gaze landed on a trail of Cora's cream running down her labia. She bent down and licked the trail of Cora's desire.

Cora cried out, arching her back.

Addy's wolf howled, getting a better taste than what they had gotten earlier.

"More," Cora moaned.

Addy held back a grin. She turned and gave a gentle nip to Cora's inner thigh.

"Be patient, my little witch. We have all night."

Cora made a frustrated sound at the back of her throat. Her chest was rising and falling fast, and her eyes were wild with fire as she waited for Addy.

Addy covered Cora's cunt with her mouth. The sound of her mate's guttural groan met her ears. It was a sound she would want to hear over and over.

The taste of Cora exploded on her tongue.

Addy was officially addicted.

She lapped up her juices while exploring every part of Cora's center. It didn't take her long to figure out what made Cora moan louder.

Addy made her way to Cora's swollen nub, latching on to it. Cora's bellow filled the air. She teased her mate unmercifully, focusing on her clit.

Cora's cries turned into pleading.

Addy's chest swelled with the notion that it was her bringing this much pleasure to Cora. She didn't ever want to move. She would prefer to stay here forever.

Addy pushed two fingers inside Cora's core, and

her tongue continued to focus on her clit. Cora must have already been close to ecstasy because soon, Addy was reward with her mate's toe-curling scream.

Cora's slick channel clamped down on Addy's fingers, and her body arched off the couch. Her sweet cream flowed from her. Addy ensured that she caught it all.

Cora's breath was ragged, and she collapsed against the cushions. Her eyes were closed, and there was a fine sheen of sweat coating her body.

Addy released her clit and withdrew her fingers.

Cora's eyes opened and met Addy's gaze. A moan slipped from her as she took in Addy cleaning her fingers with her tongue.

Addy stood from her perch on the floor. She helped shift Cora's position so she could slip onto the couch with her.

Her wolf demanded they take more, but for now, Addy would be satisfied with holding her mate.

Cora spun around in her arms. The couch wasn't the biggest, but it was snug with them on it. Their breasts were smushed between them, and they faced each other. Cora's skin was still flushed from her climax.

"We aren't done yet," Cora said, her eyes flashing a mischievous glint.

Addy bent down and covered her mouth with hers in a sweet, deep kiss. Cora's arms wound their way around her neck, holding her close.

"We are for now," Addy said gently. She brushed the dark hair from Cora's face, tucking the strands behind her ear.

"But you didn't get to—"

"We have plenty of time for that," Addy breathed. She ran a hand along Cora's back. Once she fully mated with her, there would be no holding her back from claiming her in the way of her people.

But before they went that far, she needed to know what Cora was hiding from her. Her wolf didn't like knowing their mate was potentially in danger. She was already coming up with a plan. They would go to the enforcers and the alpha to seek protection for her.

Evan Gerwulf, the alpha of the Nightstar Pack, was an honorable and reasonable wolf. He would listen to Cora and offer the protection of the pack.

She was sure of it. There was no way he would leave a female to be harmed.

Not one who was the mate of a member of his pack.

Addy needed Cora to have full trust in her. They may have only just met, but they were meant to be. Both of them felt what fate had in store for them, but if they were going to completely bond with each other, then Cora had to trust her.

And the first step would be telling Addy everything.

"Why the sudden change?" Cora asked. Her bright-blue eyes were wide and focused on Addy. Her hand slid along Addy's hip. "When we were in the woods, you were ready to pounce on me."

A growl vibrated in Addy's chest at the memory of their meeting. She still couldn't believe her wolf had rushed Cora. She would never harm a hair on her mate's head, but her wolf had got so excited at being near Cora that she'd slammed into her, going full speed.

Had Cora been a human, she might have been injured.

But her wolf just ended up loving on Cora, licking her face and sniffing her.

Her wolf could be a vicious animal, but when it came down to her mate, she was a big teddy bear.

"Maybe you were right. Let's get to know each

other." She glanced down at Cora whose expression gave away that she didn't believe a word Addy said.

But it would have to do for now.

Until then, she would have no problems pleasuring her mate to orgasm.

Cora was filled with wonder and excitement. She couldn't believe that she had her soul mate standing next to her. She and Addy had finally dragged themselves off the couch after both of their stomachs made themselves known.

"Don't let it burn. Keep stirring while I take care of the noodles," Cora instructed.

"I know how to cook," Addy grumbled. She carefully stirred the homemade Alfredo sauce that Cora had thrown together.

Cora had slid her tunic back on when they had begun cooking their meal. Addy, being the shifter, had insisted on remaining naked while cooking.

Not that Cora didn't appreciate being able to view Addy, but it was a little distracting. It was fun sharing the duties of preparing their meal. Cora loved to cook, and when she was back home, she would always find reasons to make big meals for her family.

Ever since she had felt her knowing awaken inside her, she was constantly aroused. The memory of that mind-blowing orgasm she'd had on the couch still lingered in her head.

Cora tried to push it out of her mind. She slid her hands in the oven mitts and picked up the pot with the fettuccine noodles and poured it into the colander in the sink. She sat the pot back on the stove and rinsed the noodles with cold water. She turned around and leaned back against the counter, unable to take her gaze off Addy.

Her core grew slick again. She was unable to hide this from Addy. It would only take a few seconds before her shifter nose picked up on Cora's scent.

Cora bit her lip at the memory of seeing Addy kneeling before her with her face buried between her legs. She couldn't even remember the last time she'd had an orgasm because of someone else, much less one that had rocked her world the way it did.

It had to be the knowing.

Cora loved sex just like the next person, but she

didn't walk around on the edge of an orgasm every day.

Addy's nose flared slightly. She glanced over at Cora, a growl escaping her.

It was a complete turn-on that she knew Cora was aroused with one sniff, or how her eyes glowed when her animal was close, or how wide her tongue felt sliding through her slick folds—

Cora closed her eyes tight, trying to will her body to calm down. Her core pulsed with an intense need, and if she wasn't careful, she'd climax right there just by looking at Addy.

"This sauce is done," Addy announced. She flipped the stove off and faced Cora. Her eyes did their wolf thing. She took the few steps to Cora and trapped her against the sink.

"What are you thinking about?" Addy's eyebrows arched high. The corner of her lips curved up slightly.

She knew.

"Nothing." Cora cleared her throat.

Addy closed the gap between them, her body molding to Cora's. She leaned in to where her lips brushed Cora's earlobe.

"Now why would you lie to me, witch?" Addy whispered.

A shiver overtook Cora's body.

"You know I can scent how wet your pussy is for me," Addy said.

A moan slipped from Cora. It was hard for her to take in a deep breath. The tension surrounding them was so thick.

Would it always be this way?

"Addy," she whimpered.

Addy's hand dove into Cora's thick hair, her fingers slightly massaging her scalp. Goosebumps popped up on Cora's skin. Her body was no longer under her control. The second Addy touched her, all lucid thoughts went out the window.

"Let me ease that ache between your legs," Addy murmured.

Cora's knees threatened to buckle. She reached out and held on to Addy's waist.

Goddess, she loved it when Addy talked dirty to her.

"But we just made dinner."

Addy pulled back and stared at her with hooded eyes. Cora's gaze dropped down to Addy's mouth remembering how much pleasure it had brought her.

"You have a microwave. We can always heat it

up later." Addy covered Cora's mouth in a heated kiss.

The desire pooling inside her grew.

Addy dominated the kiss. Her tongue pushed its way into Cora's mouth, stroking hers. Cora leaned into the kiss, not wanting it to end. Her nipples pebbled beneath her shirt. As if sensing what she needed, Addy reached up with her claws bared and sliced Cora's shirt from her body. The cotton material floated to the floor.

The second her breasts rubbed against Addy's, Cora was a goner.

Addy knelt before her. She lifted Cora's leg and settled it on her shoulder. She covered Cora's pussy with her mouth and went to work.

Cora threw her head back as a cry escaped her.

Yes, they could always heat up the food later.

Chapter Seven

C ora slowly opened her eyes to the sensation of something tugging at her breast. She stiffened for a moment, but then it all came rushing back to her.

Addy.

Their night together.

After orgasm number two, they had heated up their food and ate it together on the couch. Cora had been alone for so long that it was just nice to have someone to talk with. Once they were done with their meal, they tag teamed cleaning the kitchen.

Addy insisted that she stay the night with Cora. She wasn't going to argue. They had pulled down the Murphy bed and put on the clean sheets that were provided for her. A quick shower ended with Cora having orgasm number three.

Cora released a sigh.

Throughout the night, Addy had been relentless. Cora had stopped counting after orgasm five. The woman loved to have her face buried between her thighs.

Cora's body had become mush, and finally Addy had allowed her to sleep.

Cora opened her eyes and found Addy suckling on her breast. Cora reached down and brushed her red hair from her skin, admiring her beauty.

"Good morning," Cora murmured.

Addy's eyes fluttered open. Her amber ones met Cora's. She released Cora and offered her a wide grin.

"Morning." Addy shifted higher in the bed. She pulled Cora toward her and claimed her lips in a steamy kiss. Heat radiated from Addy's body. Even though the air-conditioner in the apartment kept it cool while outside's temperatures were raising.

The sensation of Addy's soft, curvy body rubbing against hers was heaven.

I could get used to waking up like this.

Cora's heart stuttered.

She was going to have to come clean with Addy.

Things were moving entirely too fast, but this was the way the knowing occurred.

There was no way she could continue being around her and not tell her that she was on the run.

The goddess had blessed her with a mate, and Cora would do what she needed to protect Addy.

Cora pulled away from Addy. Already, her heart ached at the thought of something happening to Addy. She would never forgive herself.

"What's wrong?" Addy asked. Concern lined her face as she watched Cora carefully.

Addy slid her foot along Cora's calf. The action was innocent, but it was enough to send a ripple of desire through her.

The knowing inside Cora flared. It was awakening again, and right now, this was not the time for her to act on her carnal desires.

"I'm from Washington," Cora blurted out. It was like a weight lifted from her shoulders with the admission. Last night, Addy had kept her entertained about stories of her growing up in Howling Valley.

"The state?"

Cora nodded. Nervously, she reached up and trailed a finger across Addy's collarbone. It skated down along Addy's sternum.

"There is a very good reason I'm keeping my powers hidden," she admitted. This was going to be hard for her to openly share what she'd had to deal with for so long.

But she had her mate.

It took a lot of power to muffle her majestic energy.

If she dropped her guard, Derwin would know where she was.

Addy patiently waited for her to continue.

"If you aren't ready to tell me—"

"No, I want to." Cora blew out a shaky breath. She couldn't think straight with Addy constantly trying to touch her. Cora climbed out of the bed and walked over to the dresser where she had stored some of her clothes. She didn't have much, but she had managed to pack a nightshirt. She took it out and put it on before turning around to face Addy.

"I'm listening," Addy said. She sat up in the bed and leaned back against the pillows, watching her with those glowering eyes. A low growl filled the air.

Addy scowled at Cora's shirt.

Her wolf shifter preferred her in her au naturel state.

Wrapping her arms around herself, Cora leaned against the wall, needing to get this off of her chest.

"I was raised in the small town of Oceana, Washington. It's located right on the Pacific Ocean. I come from a family of witches and warlocks. My parents were soul mates, lucky enough to have found each other. From their union they had my elder brother, Marden, and me. We lived in peace, belonging to the local coven, Oasis Moon." Her gaze flicked to Addy who was listening intently.

Addy remained quiet. She and her wolf must have understood that Addy needed to share her story.

"From a young age, our former priestess had taken me under her wing. She must have seen things in me. She worked with me, training me to use my talents that were a blessing from the goddess above. Under her guidance, I became a healer. There are many other talents I have, but she and my parents grew worried about me. I was then taught to suppress my gifts."

Cora walked over to the edge of the bed and sat.

"Why? If you were talented enough to have your coven leader train you?"

"Because not only did I gain her attention, but from others as well. A year ago, our beloved priestess died. Her nephew was to ascend as the next to lead our great coven."

"What did she die from?" Addy whispered.

Cora closed her eyes, great sorrow filling her. Brumelda had been like a grandmother to her. She still missed her to this day. The sight of her lying on the fire pyre before they'd lit the embers still came to mind. Her long gray hair had circled her hair like a cloud.

She had been given an honorable burial.

Warm tears scalded Cora's cheeks. Her hands were clenched together in her lap as she thought of the lies that were spread.

"They proclaimed it to be natural causes. Brumelda had to be close to one hundred years old, but she was in perfect health." Cora wiped the tears away. She would be strong for Brumelda's memory. She would one day avenge her. "My friend, Topaz, a seer, called on the spirits. She was able to perform a spell that most are unable to do. With my help, she was able to connect with the spirit of my beloved priestess."

"And?" Addy whispered.

"She was poisoned," Cora snapped, pain spreading through her chest. She clenched her hands into fists. A surge of an electrical current rushed down to her hands. She held them up, opening them, revealing small balls of red energy floating from her palms. "Her nephew played with dark magic, but the council didn't believe the protests from members of the coven. He was granted the leadership position of the coven."

"Okay, so you didn't want to belong to a coven turning dark," Addy stated.

Cora closed her hands, extinguishing the energy balls. She glanced over at Addy, a sad smile on her lips.

"Derwin wanted me. He knew my strength, had watched his aunt train me and understood that I was more powerful than him," Cora elaborated. "He wanted to use me to open a portal and harvest powers from the dark realm."

Addy gasped.

There was only one way she could truly explain to Addy why Derwin wanted her. She stood from the bed and faced her soul mate.

This was a risk she had to take to make her mate understand who she was.

It was going to be tricky, but she would try to keep it contained to just her apartment.

Closing her eyes, she released her powers.

* * *

A ddy's breath was snatched from her. Cora stood before her, revealing her true self. Her dark hair levitated in the air, but there was no wind blowing in the apartment. Her hands glowed the red energy she had demonstrated moments before.

The hair on the back of Addy's neck rose. Her animal stood to attention, watching their mate.

Cora opened her eyes, and her bright blues were now luminous.

"Oh my," Addy murmured. She blinked, realizing her mate was risking being noticed by showing her how powerful she was. "Wait, stop. You just said that revealing your true powers would notify your coven leader?"

Addy scrambled from the bed and stopped in front of Cora. She didn't know if she could touch her with the amount of energy sizzling from her.

"It's okay. I'm controlling it. I constructed a ward around my place, so that way my energy trails would remain here amongst us."

In a blink of an eye, Cora was back to her normal self.

Addy stood in awe. She gently reached up to cup Cora's face. This was her amazing mate.

Powerful.

Beautiful.

And she was on the run for her life, because some asshat wanted to claim her as his own to use her.

Addy's chest rumbled. She moved closer to Cora and pulled her against her. Cora wrapped her arms around Addy, burying her face into the crook of Addy's neck. Tremors racked Cora's body, her hold on Addy tightening.

"It's okay. I'm here for you," Addy promised. She pressed a kiss to Cora's temple. "I will do everything in my power to protect you."

Cora lifted her head, tears in her eyes, a small smile on her lips.

"I know. It just felt so good to be able to share this with someone. I've been on my own since I ran."

"What of your family?"

Addy guided Cora down to sit on the bed. She kept an arm wrapped around Cora's waist to allow her to lean on her.

Her wolf prowled around inside her chest. She sensed their mate was in need of comfort.

Addy didn't like to see Cora in tears. She vowed

to do what she must to always put a smile on Cora's face.

"My parents were able to help me escape, but my brother..." Cora paused, staring off into space as if reliving a moment.

Addy gently stroked Cora's hair away from her face.

Cora faced her with tormented eyes. "My brother turned against me. He sided with Derwin. I don't know what happened to my parents or if Derwin and Marden knew they helped me escape."

Addy's wolf grew ferocious. How could a brother turn on his sister? Addy thought of the bond she had with her siblings and couldn't fathom either of them turning on each other.

"We need to speak with the alpha. He will know what to do," Addy said confidently.

"I couldn't bring your pack into this mess," Cora said fiercely.

Addy grinned at her mate. She was cute when she was fired up.

"It's a little too late for this, my little witch." Addy chuckled. She tipped Cora's face to hers. "The second my eyes landed on you, your problem became mine."

Addy kissed her. She meant what she'd said, they would protect Cora.

Cora broke the kiss, staring at Addy.

"And just because you ask, they will?" she asked in disbelief.

"The alpha will hold his monthly pack audience where we can go to him."

Cora bit her lip, before seeming to come to terms with the plan.

Addy wanted to take all of the worry from her mate. "That audience is tonight. We will go, and then everything will be fine."

Cora relaxed. "Why don't I make us something to eat?"

Addy's wolf growled, but food wasn't what she had in mind. She had spent a perfectly good night with her face buried between Cora's thighs.

But, she did need to allow her mate to eat.

"Whatever you want to make is fine." Addy stood from the bed and leaned over to drop a kiss on Cora's forehead. "While you do that, mind if I get in the shower?"

"But of course." Cora hopped up from the bed, appearing as if she needed to have something to do to keep her mind occupied.

Addy grabbed her arm and forced her to turn

to face her. "I still want you to move in with me." She wasn't going to budge on this. Her mate should be with her. She wasn't going to let up on this topic until she got her way.

"I'll think about it." A mischievous glint entered Cora's eyes, then she spun around and walked to the kitchenette.

Addy smirked.

Her mate was certainly stubborn.

But that was okay, she liked a challenge.

Two could play that game.

Chapter Eight

Cora closed the door behind her. Addy had called a friend of hers to drive them to pack grounds.

"Malissa is my best friend. You'll like her."

"Anyone who is a friend of yours is a friend of mine." Cora smiled.

She and Addy had spent the perfect day together. They had managed to not spend it entirely in bed. They were able to talk for hours. It had helped to remember the good memories her family had.

She didn't want to think the worst, and Addy had urged her to share with her about her childhood, learning how to wield her magic. She'd shared stories of spending summers with her parents, camping and learning to become one with nature.

Or the time when learning to utilize her energy burst, she'd set her mother's hair on fire.

Her stories had left them both in a fit of giggles.

It had been therapeutic for her.

This is what it feels like to have your other half with you.

Cora tucked her key into the side pocket of her bag and followed Addy down the stairs. Butterflies filled her gut at the thought of meeting someone Addy was close with. If this woman who was picking them up was her best friend, then she would know all about Addy, the good and the bad.

"Are you sure she won't mind picking us up?" Cora asked.

They exited the side door to the garage and headed down the driveway to the street. Chuck's truck wasn't in the yard, signaling he wasn't home. If what Addy said was true, then it was best he didn't see Addy here.

There was no way one could not know she was a shifter. The color of her eyes and the way she walked was obvious she was part animal.

A white sedan was parked on the street with the engine running.

"I'm sure. She's going to get a kick out of meeting you." Addy grinned. She grabbed Cora's hand and towed her behind her. "Come on. She won't bite. I promise."

Cora was going to put her trust in Addy. She had wanted to lay low while in town and slowly submerge herself into the town and get to know people.

But that would not be the case anymore.

Addy was taking her right before the alpha to pour out her troubles and ask for refuge in their town.

They arrived near the car. Addy opened the back door and helped Cora enter. Addy slid in behind her.

"What am I, a taxi service?" A beautiful blonde sat in the driver's seat. She grinned and turned around to face them.

"Just drive." Addy chuckled.

"I'm not sure you can afford my prices." Malissa snorted.

"Oh, I can. I'm sure you wouldn't want me telling your mother what really happened to her bed of tulips," Addy threatened.

"You wouldn't dare." She narrowed her eyes on

Addy before focusing on Cora. "Hello, I'm Malissa."

"Cora," Cora replied, offering a small smile. She instantly sensed the sisterly love between the two.

"Nice to meet you. It would appear I'm your local taxi. Buckle up, I'll have to you Addy's house in no time."

Malissa threw the car in drive, and they were off.

Cora's body jerked back against the seat. At the speed Malissa was driving, she hurriedly put her seat belt on. She watched the scenery fly by. The area of Howling Valley was absolutely gorgeous. The townsfolk certainly took pride in their homes.

Cora couldn't wait to explore it more.

Soon, they were driving away from the town. Open land and plenty of trees surrounded them.

Cora glanced forward and met Malissa's eyes in the rearview mirror.

"So you're the reason my friend hasn't been home in a day." Malissa grinned.

Cora's face warmed. She glanced over at Addy who was smiling.

"Leave her be," Addy murmured. She entwined her fingers with Cora's and brought her hand up to her lips, pressing a soft kiss to it. "She's new to town and—"

"Obviously your mate," Malissa mused. She took a left turn that had Cora's body falling into Addy's.

"That she is," Addy confirmed. Something was shared between the two of them. A look, and it almost seemed if they were communicating with each other telepathically.

Cora was sure Malissa had questions but didn't want to ask in front of her.

"What do you have planned tonight? Anything fun?" Malissa asked.

"We are going to the alpha's audience," Addy announced. She squeezed Cora's hand as if to reassure her.

"Is something wrong?"

"There were some issues in Cora's last town, and we just want to ask for protection for her. She's now going to be calling Howling Valley home—"

"She's not a shifter," Malissa interrupted.

"I know, but you know the alpha will protect any paranormal who needs help," Addy said firmly.

"I can't sense what you are." Malissa curiously glanced at Cora again in the mirror.

"I'm a witch. I'm suppressing my powers at the

moment," Cora admitted.

The confusion in Malissa's eyes cleared up.

"Some power you got there. Had I not known, I would have assumed you were human." Malissa shrugged. They drove in a comfortable silence for a while, then Malissa broke the silence. "We can probably cancel the trip over to Grove Hill?"

Addy cleared her throat, her cheeks growing flushed this time. Cora's eyebrows rose. She had yet to see her soul mate appear embarrassed.

It was downright cute.

"We can still go. I'm hearing they are going to have a Treasure Hunt later after the pack festivities," Addy said.

"Oh, a Treasure Hunt? You should have led with that the other day when you brought up us going." Malissa danced in her seat. She slowed the car and turned on to a long winding dirt road.

Within a few minutes they were pulling up to a small cottage.

"Here we are," Addy murmured. She appeared nervous as she glanced from her home to Cora. "Thanks, bestie. I'll call you later about going to Grove Hill."

"Alrighty." Malissa waved. "It was nice meeting you, Cora."

"Same to you." Cora returned her smile.

Addy opened the door and slid out, helping Cora out of the car.

Cora took advantage of Addy speaking with her friend and scanned the area around them. She took in the well-manicured yard. The white structure with the dark-navy shutters.

A warm feeling spread through her chest as she gazed upon Addy's home. The road she lived on was a long one with houses lining it. It reminded her of a gated community. All of the homes were similar in structure but differed by color.

"Are you okay?" Addy asked, coming to stand next to Cora. She was dressed in Cora's borrowed clothing. Before they went to meet with the alpha, she wanted to grab her own garments. She was slightly thinner than Cora, so they were a little loose on her.

"Yes, just looking around."

"Come. Let me show you my home." Addy took her hand and tugged her behind her. She led her to the door and opened it.

"You don't lock your doors?" Cora scoffed.

"What for? If someone comes here while I'm gone, I'll be able to scent them when I come back." Addy laughed. Made sense, since all shifters had crazy abilities when it came to smells. "Plus, when I had left, I thought I was going out for a short run."

She tossed a wink Cora's way.

Her heart skipped a beat, and she stepped over the threshold of Addy's home. Immediately, a sense of belonging washed over Cora. It had been a long time since she had felt completely comfortable somewhere.

"Welcome to my home." Addy brushed past her and waved for her to follow. She turned around and took Cora's hand. "Our home."

"Addy..."

"Look. You don't belong at Chuck's house. Your place is here with me."

"But what if I can't stay in Howling Valley?"

"No one is going to send you away," Addy growled. She stepped closer to Cora, closing the gap between them. She reached up and grasped Cora by the back of her neck. She leaned forward, nuzzling her face into the crook of Cora's neck. She pressed a hot kiss to her skin, teasing Cora with the edges of her fangs. "I want to put my claiming mark right here."

Cora whimpered. Her knees grew weak from Addy tormenting her. She nipped at Cora's skin.

"Addy," she breathed.

"Soon, I will mark you as mine," Addy promised. She trailed her tongue up the column of Cora's neck until she reached her ear. She tugged on it with her teeth.

The movement sent a tremor through Cora.

The knowing inside her flared to life.

It was growing stronger.

Demanding she bind herself to this wolf.

In the throes of passion, she would pledge herself to this wolf, binding them together.

Forever.

It sounded divine, but there was one problem.

Cora was scared.

What if Derwin found her? He'd punish her for running. He wouldn't hurt her, for he needed her, but he wouldn't think twice about harming someone she cared about.

Cora drew back from Addy.

"What's wrong?" Addy asked. Her brow furrowed together, and she stared at her.

"Nothing. If we are to make it to the audience with the alpha, we best get going."

Addy paused, not taking her eyes off her for a moment. She relaxed and took Cora's hand.

"The tour won't take long. This place isn't that big." Addy grinned. She tugged Cora behind her, walking her through the living room which was cozy with oversized couches.

Cora eyed them, imagining having lazy days with Addy.

Snuggled up together, in front of the television watching movies.

That was exactly what she could see her and Addy doing. Her chest ached with the vision.

Addy towed her behind her toward the kitchen. It was state of the art and beautiful. They moved on throughout the house. They finally ended in Addy's bedroom.

The colors of the room were warm, and again, that comfy feeling settled inside Cora. She glanced at the bed, and her breath hitched in her throat.

The king-sized bed was high off the floor, with a thick blanket covering the mattress while six throw pillows were carefully placed.

She just wanted to jump onto the bed and never leave.

"Let me change into my clothes and we'll be going," Addy said. She released Cora, going over to her walk-in closet. She disappeared into the little room.

"You do have a lovely home," Cora said. She didn't want to seem too eager to like her house.

ARIEL MARIE

What if the alpha didn't want her to stay? She didn't want to get too attached to Addy.

What are you talking about?

It was already too late. The knowing had awakened inside her, and it wouldn't settle down until she had bound herself to Addy.

She walked around the room, taking in the pictures in frames that were spread around the room before heading into the attached bathroom.

Marble floors, a glass-encased shower, and a white clawfoot tub gave Cora a reason to pause.

This bathroom was everything she would have hoped for.

Even the toilet had a small room inside the en suite.

She blew out a shaky breath and went back int the bedroom just as Addy came out of the closet.

"Is the house to your pleasing?" Addy asked. She took Cora's hand and placed a kiss to the back of it. "If there is anything you would want changed, we can do it. My brother's friend is a contractor and helped me design everything."

"What? Oh, no. I couldn't." Cora shook her head.

"I'm going to convince you. Just watch and see." Addy smiled and pressed a kiss to Cora's cheek.

Chapter Nine

Addy didn't want to take her hand off Cora. Deep down, she felt if she did, her mate would disappear.

She didn't think Cora would leave, but whenever she brought up the subject of Cora moving in with her, Cora became skittish. Addy had to convince her to move in with her. Living apart wouldn't be good for them. Her animal was already growing impatient. It was time for them to claim their mate.

They walked along peacefully down the path to the community building. There weren't many people out at this time of day. It was late afternoon, and the temperature was decreasing to something more comfortable.

Addy took a peek at Cora who was dressed in her long flowing skirt, sandals, and a shirt that was snug to her body. Her midnight hair flowed past her shoulders. Addy was struck by her natural beauty.

"Is there anything I should expect?" Cora asked quietly.

"No. We are going to officially notify the alpha you are in town," Addy began.

Cora stiffened, but Addy hurried on to calm her down.

"He will need to know about you and what you are dealing with. That is how he will protect not only you, but the town."

"I just don't understand why he would go through those lengths to help someone who is not from around here, doesn't belong to your pack, and may cause more harm than good," Cora said. Her shoulders slumped as if she had already given up.

"That's what we do around here." Addy brought them to a halt and forced Cora to look at her. She had to make her see that she was going to be safe here. No one was going to mess with her mate while she had breath in her body. "No one should have to look over their shoulders their entire life. That is no way to live. Your knowing has identified me as your soul mate, while my wolf knows you are mine. We are going to do this together."

Cora's wide eyes filled with tears. She smiled softly and leaned into Addy who wrapped her arms around her.

"You are one stubborn wolf." Cora chuckled.

Addy smiled and tightened her arms around her mate.

"You just don't know."

Cora stepped back, blowing out a deep breath. "Let's go do this."

Addy nodded and led the way. The path broke out into a clearing where the community center was located. It was the building where a lot of the pack business was conducted. There were a few cars in the parking lot, possibly members of the pack who did not live on their private grounds.

They made their way to the building where Lupe, one of the enforcers, stood on guard.

"Addy." Lupe nodded to her. His curious gaze landed on Cora. His nostrils flared slightly.

"Hey, Lupe. This is Cora." She quickly made introductions. "She's new to town, and I need to take her to meet with the alpha."

"Is something wrong?" It was amazing how intuitive he was on things.

Addy knew that was what made him a great enforcer. His piercing eyes never missed a thing.

"Small problem, but nothing the alpha can't fix." She took Cora's hand and practically dragged her inside before he started with more questions. Cora's magic was being suppressed. Like Malissa, he would sense there was more to Cora, but would be left assuming she was human.

"Are all the enforcers intense like him?" Cora whispered.

"Yes and no."

Addy guided them through the foyer and down a hallway to the room where the alpha would be meeting with the public. They walked past a couple of activity rooms and a large conference room. Most of the pack business when everyone was gathered took place outside in the back.

There were two people standing in line outside the alpha's room. Addy blew out a sigh of relief that they wouldn't have to wait long.

Griffin and Jatix, additional enforcers, stood outside the room. They were both large men, who were dedicated to the alpha and the pack.

Griffin took notice of Addy and smiled.

"Hey, Addy! Didn't I see you at the wedding?" he asked.

"Yes, Bess and I were there." She grinned. He was the elder brother of Robin, the wolf shifter who'd married her human mate. Bess and Robin were friends who had graduated from high school together. "That was some reception. We had a great time."

"Good. My mother had us running around like crazy to make sure everything went off without a hitch." He shook his head but was all smiles. Everyone knew how protective Griffin was of his younger sibling.

"Where did they go? I heard they went on a honeymoon?" Shifters normally did not have a wedding. A mating was private between couples. It wasn't too uncommon for a party to be held to celebrate the fated union.

"Aruba. The pictures Robin has texted me are gorgeous."

A couple exited the room. Jatix motioned for the couple ahead of them to enter.

"Who's your friend." Griffin nodded to Cora who had remained silent.

Addy turned to find her quietly watching their conversation.

"This is Cora. She's new to town." Addy hesitated on whether or not she should introduce Cora as her mate. They hadn't talked about that yet. As much as her wolf wanted to howl to the world she had found her destined other half, she held off. She made a note to speak with Cora about their relationship and what they were going to do about it.

She couldn't wait forever. Her wolf would drive her nuts if she didn't. Wolves who had met their mates and did not claim them would go crazy and unstable. There were rumors of a wolf who had to be locked up by the alpha because he went feral when he couldn't claim his mate.

The hairs on the back of Addy's neck stood to attention. Her animal prowled inside her.

That would be Addy.

She would go insane if she didn't get to sink her teeth into Cora's flesh and claim her.

"Hello," Cora murmured. She turned her big blue eyes to Griffin and Jatix who were watching her.

"Welcome to Howling Valley." Griffin gave her a smile. "If you've made friends with Addy, I'm sure she'll show you around and get you real comfortable here."

Addy held back a smirk. He just didn't know how much she'd been making Cora comfortable.

"Thank you." Cora returned his smile.

"Where are you from?" Jatix asked, tilting his head to the side. He was quietly studying her.

Addy tried to offer Cora strength. It was apparent she was uncomfortable with the attention.

Addy didn't know what her mate had been through since she'd escaped her coven, and couldn't even imagine.

One thing she knew, was she was going to make sure Cora never wanted to leave.

"From up north," Cora replied.

"Hmmm…" Jatix didn't take his eyes off her.

"How's everything been going, Jatix?" Addy tried to distract the brooding wolf.

He glanced at her and gave a shrug.

"Nothing I can complain about," he replied.

"Doesn't seem like many people will be coming today." Addy looked around. The center was pretty quiet. There were normally a lot of people bustling through holding meetings, events, and elders going to Bingo night.

"Tomorrow the building is going to undergo some slight renovations. So they moved some of the activities to town at the library and church," Jatix said.

Soon the shifter couple exited the room.

"Go ahead in, Addy." Griffin nodded to the room.

Addy's heart sped up.

It was their turn.

Cora focused her round eyes to her and reached for her hand again.

"It's going to be okay. I promise." She led them into the room where the alpha sat in his large chair with the beta, Mick, sitting next to him. The two of them made a powerful team, and both really cared for their pack.

Taking an audience with the alpha was informal. Members of Nightstar were to go to their leader with any problems or requests.

Evan, the alpha, was a generational leader. It was his ancestors who had started their close-knit pack. He was a tall, muscular man who intimidated many upon their first meeting with him. He was a fierce wolf who was extremely protective of his wolves.

Mick was a close friend of Evan's who had accepted the position when Evan had taken over Nightstar. He was also tall, muscular with blond hair that flowed around his shoulders. He was one of the most intelligent men Addy knew.

"Adelina. I can't remember the last time you've

taken advantage of an audience with your alpha."
Evan offered her a grin. He settled back in his chair
and folded his arms across his chest.

Addy grew sheepish remembering the last time
she'd shown up to meet with her alpha. She had
been about ten years old and appeared demanding
a water park for the kids. The town pool was always
overrun by teenagers who never allowed the
younger kids the chance to swim.

Addy had arrived, requesting the alpha's ear.

He had granted a water park for the town's
children.

"Hello, Alpha. Beta." She nodded to both of
them. "May I introduce you to Cora Latimer. She's
recently moved to Howling Valley."

"Hello." Cora stood to her full height and met
their curious gazes.

"When are you claiming her as your mate?"
Evan asked. His gaze flickered between the two of
them.

Addy should have known.

The alpha knew everything.

Addy glanced at Cora then turned back to her
alpha and beta with a shrug. Her smile disappeared
as she cleared her throat.

"Well, we have a problem," she began.

Drawing in a deep breath, she explained how Cora came to be at Howling Valley, their connection, and what Cora had shared with her.

Evan and Mick did not utter a word. They listened intently, absorbing the information.

Finally, Addy went silent.

"What is the name of your coven?" Evan asked. All hints of joking were gone from the alpha. The tension in the room was palpable.

"Oasis Moon," Cora replied.

"I've heard about an unrest out of Washington. A coven being overturned, fighting each other," Mick murmured.

"We need to alert the enforcers and up security," Evan growled. He stood to his full height and walked toward Addy and Cora. His golden eyes were burning bright. His attention was focused on Cora. "Rest well, Cora Latimer. I can feel the connection between you and Adelina. The mate of one of my wolves makes you an honorary member of our pack."

"That is very kind of you, sir. But Derwin is psychotic and will do anything in his power to take me back—"

She was interrupted by a growl echoing through

the air. Addy's wolf was sharing how she felt about anyone coming for her mate.

No one would take Cora from her.

All eyes landed on Addy. She cleared her throat, trying to get her animal to back down. She was being pushy, demanding to be let out.

"So he just wants you to return to your town and claim you?" Evan asked.

Cora shook her head. "No, sir. I mean, he does, but it's more than that. He wants to tap into my powers and use them for dark. He's evil and wants me to help him gain more power."

"How can he do that?" Addy asked quietly. Nausea filled her. She wasn't sure she wanted to know the answer.

"There is a ritual that hasn't been used in over five hundred years. By performing it, the caster can syphon powers from a witch." Cora paused. She tucked her thick hair behind her ear. "It was forbidden. No witch should drain the energy of another."

"That sounds dangerous," Mick said.

Addy watched Cora, who wouldn't look at her. She sensed there was more to the ritual than what Cora was sharing with them.

"It is very dangerous. Derwin cannot handle what is inside me." Cora finally looked at Addy.

What Addy saw in her eyes confirmed it. Her mate was not being completely forward with the information she knew.

"We can handle a crazed warlock," Evan assured them.

Relief filled Addy. Just as she knew, the alpha would extend his protection to Cora.

"But wolves don't practice magic—"

"Let us handle the Oasis Moon. We have our own local coven that is our ally. Once we tell them of a witch in need, they won't hesitate to help."

Cora froze, swallowing audibly. She glanced down at the floor and let out a sigh. The air grew thick. Addy's heart raced from the adrenaline coursing through her.

What's going on?

"I won't need the help of a coven." Cora's luminous eyes met them. A gentle breeze floated past her, but there were no open windows. Cora's hair gently lifted, floating in the air. "I'm sorry, Addy, but I didn't share with you my true strength. I'm just afraid if I unleash everything, I'll hurt people, and I can't have that on my conscience."

Addy was in awe of her mate. She wasn't upset that Cora had held back. It was understandable with the situation going on. Addy was disappointed that her mate felt she couldn't protect her.

"Don't worry about it," Addy uttered. She could feel the electricity in the air. Her wolf slammed against her chest, wanting to go to their mate. Her attraction to Cora was growing.

She needed to complete the mating bond.

Cora reached out and cupped Addy's face. "I can't risk losing you."

"You won't." Addy shook her head fiercely.

Cora's hand dropped to her side as she turned back to the alpha and beta.

"Whether or not you are more powerful than your coven, we have a duty to protect Howling Valley. I don't want this Derwin harming innocent people." Evan rested his hands on his waist. A muscle in his jaw ticked slightly. "Do they know where you are?"

"Not yet, but I have a feeling they are closing in on finding me," Cora admitted.

"Then we will still increase security," Evan snapped.

"Don't worry, Alpha. We will have eyes everywhere. All outsiders will be questioned." Mick walked over to stand by them.

"If they come, I will lead the fight away from Howling Valley," Cora vowed.

The air around them grew still. Her hair settled back along her shoulders. Cora blinked, her eyes returning to their normal bright-blue orbs.

She turned to Addy and took her hands. "When this happens, promise me you'll run—"

"No." Addy would never run from a fight involving her mate. Her wolf wouldn't allow that. Her beast was already ready to defend their mate.

"I mean it, Addy. I can't have them hurt you," Cora pleaded.

"We'll cross that bridge when it comes," Evan interjected. He glanced at Cora. "She's a wolf, and running away from someone threatening her mate would never happen."

Cora's shoulders slumped.

"What I would suggest, is stay together. Report anything out of the ordinary. Enjoy each other," Mick suggested. "We are a powerful pack. If your coven believes they will come here to take you against your will, they have another think coming."

"Mick is right. Leave everything to us," Evan said. "Addy, take her around and make sure she enjoys our town. This is her home now."

Chapter Ten

Cora stepped into her sandals and grabbed her keys. Her small bag rested on her shoulder with the few items she would need. Exiting her apartment, she jogged down the stairs and slipped through the door. Cora headed to the woods behind her home.

Addy had tried to talk her into moving in with her again, but Cora wasn't quite ready yet. There were some things she had to put in place before she would feel comfortable living with Addy.

If Derwin found her, then she didn't want him to know about Addy.

He would play dirty to get what he wanted from her.

She couldn't risk Addy. If something were to happen to her, Cora wouldn't handle it well.

Anyone in her path would be hurt.

It was a guarantee.

Just this quick, her knowing had already attached to Addy, making her more important to Cora than breathing.

Yesterday when they had met with the alpha and beta, she had learned something interesting.

Howling Valley had a coven.

She was tempted to reach out to them, but she wanted to check them out first. She didn't want to insult the alpha by saying she didn't trust any covens until she knew for certain they weren't in cahoots with Derwin.

On her travels, she had discovered quite a few who believed in what he was trying to achieve.

Dark magic was something dangerous.

Cora entered the woods, unafraid that it was close to midnight. She wasn't scared of anything potentially lurking out in the darkness.

They should be more afraid of her.

She hated that she had been lying to Addy about just how powerful she was. But she had to protect herself and those around her. That was why she had remained alone for so long.

She didn't want to get close to anyone.

A short time in Howling Valley, and her knowing was awakened.

With determined footsteps, Cora went deeper into the woods.

Derwin could not get his hands on her.

If he was able to perform the Torrent Sacré, mankind would be in trouble. The Torrent Sacré was one of the most forbidden spells around.

If performed correctly, Derwin could take all of her powers.

Draining a witch's power would kill her.

A witch's power was directly connected with their life's energy.

Derwin wouldn't care about her then.

He'd always had a weird fascination with her. She'd never known why until he'd taken over the throne.

Cora paused and glanced around. She had made it pretty far from her apartment. She was going to have to do something to protect Howling Valley. She was going to caste a protective ward around it.

This was going to take a lot of energy, but it would keep Derwin from entering the town.

It was going to be necessary for her to try to

protect the innocent people of Howling Valley and her soul mate.

She unzipped the bag on her shoulder and reached in for something she had kept with her. A small vial held strands of Derwin's hair.

She tried not to think of the night she'd snatched it from him.

She had been walking down the street. It had been a few days after they had performed the final death rites for Brumelda.

He'd been following her.

"Let me claim you, Cora," Derwin demanded. His gaze narrowed on her.

Cora took a step backwards. He was taller than her, with brown hair he kept long, pulled back in a ponytail at the nape of his neck. A scar ran down the right side of his face. Cora was unsure where he had gotten it from, but it marred his features. He once would have been considered handsome, but the scar gave him a hint of danger.

"What?" She blinked. Did she hear him correctly? "Claim me? Why?"

Derwin stalked toward her, closing the gap between them. He reached out to stroke her hair, but she jerked away. His sickening chuckle echoed through the air.

Something was off about him. He'd never paid much attention to her before.

Why now?

"Because I sense your raw power. You think you can hide it from me, but you can't. I know the reason my aunt has worked with you all these years."

"You do?" Her eyebrows rose. Brumelda would never share her secret. Her mentor had stressed that she could never let anyone know about her true powers. "What did she tell you?"

"It wasn't what she said to me. It's what I picked up."

"And what is that?"

"She was grooming you for me." His sadistic grin spread across his face. His hand rushed out and gripped her arm, bringing her close to him. Seriously, he was sicker than she'd thought. "I know she would want you to be my queen."

"You have lost your mind. Brumelda was training me, because she saw potential in me as a healer," she bit out through clenched teeth. She fought against his hold, trying to free her arm. "Let me go. You are hurting me."

"You can say what you want, but I know the truth."

"You are crazy!" she cried out, yanking her arm, but his hand tightened on her.

He dragged her behind a row of trees, out of sight of anyone driving by. Fear crept through her. She had to get away from him.

"You think I'm crazy?" he rasped. His brown eyes flared a bright golden hue. "You may want to rethink that. This

coven is mine now, and there are going to be a lot of changes around this place. I'm in charge now, and I can make things very easy for you."

"Why are you doing this?" An electrical current rippled through her body.

No!

She had to control herself. She couldn't let Derwin know.

"This is my destiny. I've seen it. I was meant to not only rule our coven, but the entire world. I will be the high priest of every single witch and warlock on this wretched planet." His eyes had become unfocused, but now they were staring at her with a dark intent. "You will be by my side. And this act you put on as if you are a lowly witch. Cut the bullshit. I see right through your façade. I know you are much more powerful than you share. I can feel it coursing through you now."

She continued struggling to break free. Her hand closed around strands of his hair. She tugged hard, jerking them from his head.

"You bitch!" He let her go.

Cora stumbled backwards, righting herself before she fell. Her pulse pounded in her ears. She shook her head and reversed away from him, tucking the hair into her pocket. She didn't know why, but she was sure she would have a reason to keep them.

"You don't know anything about me." Her voice shook slightly. She fought the internal battle to control her energy.

He barked a laugh that sent a tremor down her spine.

He was pure evil. She could feel it. How had the council not seen him for what he was?

"The council will know what you are," she threatened.

"Who is going to do anything about it? I am the high priest. Those old fuckers are too scared to test me." He held out a hand and leveled his gaze on her. "Come to me, Cora. Let me show you how to truly use those powers."

"No." Cora backed away.

"It wasn't a question."

He dashed toward her, but she threw up her hands.

It was the first mistake she made.

Her energy released, sending a bolt of power from her palms, slamming into him. Derwin flew backward, hitting a tree.

Cora paused in shock.

"You bitch!" he snapped.

Cora spun around and ran. She didn't dare show him anything else she could do. She raced home.

His yells still haunted her.

"I will snatch the power from you. It will be mine!"

Moon goddess above me.
Hear my plea.
Protect those around me.
Keep this evil out.

Cora knelt in the area she'd cleared out. A small candle was lit, sitting on the dirt next to her. She opened the vial with the few strands of Derwin's hair. She took one out and put the vial back in her bag.

This spell she was performing was to protect the townspeople and keep Derwin from them.

She placed the strand in the hot flame. It burned bright before turning to nothing.

No foot of his may cross my barrier.

I surround Howling Valley.

She envisioned the wards. Standing with her hands stretched out in front of her, she constructed an invisible dome to surround their area. The air was filled with the sounds of her constructing protection wards. Once it was complete, Cora opened her eyes.

No one would notice the ward. The citizens of Howling Valley could pass through it freely.

The coven Evan had spoken of may notice it. She hoped not. She would soon have to meet with them and bring them up to date on what was going on.

She risked Derwin picking up on her spell, but it was worth it. Something had to be done. She infused the construction of the wards with a spell. If any other witch noticed it, they would assume that it was a standard ward.

Not one crafted by someone on her level.

Cora could construct them on her own without spells.

Derwin was close. She could feel it. She hadn't shared with the alpha and beta that he was closing in.

Cora closed her eyes and inhaled. Using a piece of him in a spell allowed her to briefly pick up on his proximity to her. He was in California.

Thankfully the state was massive, and it would take him a while to find her.

She hoped.

If he had help, there was no telling how long until he found her.

She prayed this ward would hide this small town from Derwin. If she were successful, he'd overlook it and continue his search for her elsewhere.

But deep down, she knew that wouldn't be.

He was going to find her.

Cora bent down and blew out the candle. She tossed her belongings back into her bag. She grimaced, knowing there would be candle wax on the bottom of her bag. She'd have to get it out later.

She hefted her bag onto her shoulders and walked back toward her apartment. The moon's rays floating down felt good. Witches drew their powers from the moon.

Cora loved the outdoors and loved spending time sitting outside at night absorbing energy from the moon. It was almost better than sunbathing as the humans did.

The snapping of a twig sounded off in the distance.

Cora paused, scanning the area.

Something was out there. The woods were dark, hard to see, but the moon was guiding her. She wished she had a nose as sensitive as Addy's. Her soul mate could sniff out any scent.

Cora stiffened. She didn't sense a threat but remained still. Something was walking toward her. Soft padding could be heard.

Jerking her head toward the sound, she was met with a tall muscular figure.

"Don't be alarmed, Miss Latimer," a familiar voice called out.

Cora squinted as the male came closer. Her clenched hands relaxed when he stepped into the moonlight.

"Um, Griffin?" She prayed that was the right name. It was the enforcer from the community center who had been speaking with Addy.

"Yes, ma'am. What are you doing out here at this time of night?" he asked.

She kept her eyes level with his as he was completely naked. He must have been in his wolf form before shifting to his human form to speak with her.

"I should be asking you the same thing," she said.

"Patrolling. We were informed there was a threat against your life and we were to ensure you remain safe."

Cora's heart melted. Addy had been right. The pack would protect her. She relaxed and motioned to the moon.

"I couldn't sleep and decided to go for a walk. Beautiful moon." The lie rolled easily off her tongue. She should be worried at how easy lying came to her, but she wasn't. Had this been months ago, she wouldn't have been, but after living a life on the run, she didn't even bat an eyelid when speaking untruths.

"Where's Addy? You shouldn't be out here alone," he said.

"I'm sure she's at home. This is my home, and I live just over there." She pointed in the area of her apartment. "I'm on my property and not even far from my apartment. I just needed fresh air."

"Can I escort you back home?" he asked.

"No, I'm fine. I'm heading that way now." She backed away from him and gave him a smile, trying to act normal. "Goodnight."

"Night, Miss Latimer."

Cora sensed his eyes on her. She continued on, not looking back. She quickened her footsteps once she broke through the clearing. Her gaze landed on the garage, and she hurried along. She pulled out her key and let herself in. Locking the door, she scurried up the stairs to her apartment. Once inside, she tossed her keys in the bowl by the door. She leaned back against the door and blew out a deep breath.

That was enough excitement for tonight.

The wards were in place. They should be safe for now. She kicked off her shoes and dropped her bag onto the couch.

A yawn overtook her. She peeled her clothes off until she was naked. The Murphy bed was still down, allowing her to climb right into it. The cool sheets greeted her tired body. Constructing a ward the size of a town took a lot of work and was taxing on the body.

She rolled over, trying to find a comfortable spot. Finally, she settled down and allowed sleep to take her.

The first face she saw as darkness claimed her... Addy's.

This dream would be a good one.

Chapter Eleven

Addy was determined to win her mate over. She was also not above getting down on her knees and groveling.

Cora belonged at her home.

She left her house, jogged down the stairs. She gripped her cellphone tight in her hand as she strode to her car.

She would go to Cora's house and demand they go out on a date. Addy's wolf was desperate to see her, taste her, and hold her.

And if she had to court her, she would.

Her phone vibrated. She glanced at the screen and bit out curse.

Her brother.

She didn't have time for this but knew if she

didn't answer, he would either continue calling until she answered, or show up at her house.

That was life with an overprotective elder brother.

"Hello?" She opened the door to her sedan and got in.

"Why the attitude?" His deep chuckle greeted her.

"I'm not in the mood, Zeff. What do you want?" Her phone automatically connected to her hands-free system in the vehicle. Addy threw the car in reverse. She backed out of the small driveway and turned toward the main road. She pushed her foot down on the pedal, revving her small car up.

"Is something wrong?" he asked, his laughter fading.

"Not in so many words," she breathed. She tightened her grip on the steering wheel. She was just flabbergasted as to why Cora wouldn't move in with her. If her wolf identified her as a mate and Cora's witchy knowing sense identified Addy, then what was the problem?

Maybe this was perfecting time for her brother to call. He was happily mated and with a child on the way.

"Well, before we delve in your problem, can I at least tell you why I am calling?" he asked.

Addy's heart fluttered at her brother's request. She loved her siblings fiercely, and if he needed something, too, then she would listen. It was rare Zeff called on her with a problem. Her big brother was always there for her and Bess.

"I'm sorry, Zeffy." She sniffled. It was her nickname for him from when she was a kid. She'd idealized her siblings when she was younger. Zeffy became her name for him when she was missing her two front teeth.

"Lynne and I are expecting again," he announced proudly.

Even with the turmoil going on in her head, she couldn't help but scream for joy. Her brother and mate had wanted plenty of pups.

"That is wonderful news, Zeffy." Her grin was wide. She loved being an aunty. She was the youngest of the siblings, so it made her the coolest aunt.

"Yeah, well, I wanted to tell you first before Ma called you. I'm sure she will be soon. Lynne, Junior, and I had dinner with them last night." He laughed, but then it slowly faded. It was as if knew he needed to jump back into his protective brother role. "Now, whose ass do I have to kick?"

Addy giggled. If she went to him even at their age and said someone was picking on her, he'd go find the person and beat them to a pulp.

"No one. I'm fine." She chewed on her lip for a moment, trying to decide how to approach the subject. She'd always been able to speak with her brother about anything, so she just decided to blurt out her question. "How did you convince Lynne to accept your mating?"

The line was silent. She looked at the screen on her dashboard to see if the call had been disconnected.

Zeff coughed.

"You've found your mate?" he asked, slowly.

Addy nodded as if he could see her.

"And they don't want to mate with you?" he queried.

"She's not a shifter," Addy stated. If Cora had been, then this call would be weird. Shifters never backed down from mating. It was felt on both sides.

"Oh, well. That would be hard for me to answer since Lynne is a wolf. She felt it just as intensely as I did."

"But did you claim her immediately?"

"Actually, no. Lynne is a tease. We knew it would eventually happen, but she wanted to draw out the foreplay—"

"Okay, I'm going to stop you there." Addy shuddered. She loved her brother, but she didn't want to have that type of conversation with him. "I get the point, though."

His laughter filled her car.

"Well, you asked." He sighed. "I hope she accepts you, little sis."

"You'd like her."

"I'm sure I would. Hurry up and claim your mate before Mom catches wind your mate is in town. You wouldn't want her meddling."

"Oh, fates no," Addy groaned.

Their mother would have no problem going to Cora to try to convince her on why Addy would make a fabulous mate. She could see Clover Ransome now. Her mother had no shame in wanting all of her children mated off.

But something Zeff had said did give her an idea.

He'd admitted that Lynne wanted to prolong the foreplay...maybe that's what she had to do.

Foreplay done the right way would bring any woman to her knees. She could have Cora eating out of the palms of her hands and begging for her to claim her.

Addy's gums burned from her fangs threatening to descend.

She would have to turn on the good ol' Ransome charm and win her mate.

Addy drove through town, almost nearing the road that would take her to Cora's house. She pulled up to a stop light, catching movement at the corner.

Cora.

She stood waiting for the pedestrian light to turn green.

Addy watched her mate. Her mouth watered at the sight of her.

Cora was dressed in another long flowing dark skirt, with a sleeveless shirt. Her skin was tan, kissed by the sun. Her dark hair brushed her shoulders while she walked across the street, oblivious to Addy's stare.

When the light turned green, Addy turned the corner and headed in the direction of Cora. She pulled along the curb and rolled the passenger window down.

Cora jumped, looking her way.

"Hey, hot stuff?" Addy called out.

"Addy." Cora sauntered toward the car and leaned down into the window so they could see each other. "Where are you headed?"

"On my way to see you." Addy motioned for her to get in.

Cora opened the door and slid into the sedan. Her delicious scent filled the air. Once the door was shut, Addy rolled the window back up so the cool air wouldn't escape. It was a warm summer day, and even though Addy was a shifter who loved the outdoors, she loved central air in her car on day like this.

Addy instantly reached for Cora. "Come here."

They bent their heads to each other, sharing a short, sweet kiss.

"I missed you," Cora blurted out. Her wide eyes met Addy's.

"I missed you, too." Addy's wolf was pleased.

They stared at each other without breaking the comfortable silence. Addy had been so anxious to see her, now that she was in Cora's presence, her wolf had calmed down.

"Now tell me, where have you been?"

"I was looking for a place of employment," Cora stated matter-of-factly.

"A job? Why?" Addy was baffled. Why was she looking for a job at this time? They had just met with the alpha, explaining how her coven leader was hunting her down. Why was she worried about a job?

"Umm…because that is what people who want to be able to live and pay bills do."

Addy was about to make a joke that her mate didn't have to work if she didn't want to, but she held back. She didn't want Cora to pull back from her. Everything had been going great until Cora began to think she was a danger to Addy and the townspeople of Howling Valley.

Addy would prove to her that not only was she strong enough to defend herself, but so was her pack.

Addy was going to take it slow, court her mate, and allow the foreplay to build up until they both exploded. Cora wouldn't be able to resist what was between them.

No one could fight the draw once the fates got involved.

That would mean no more diving between Cora's legs at the moment.

Her wolf growled at the thought.

What was between Cora's thighs was meant for her tongue. Her sweet, delectable smell and taste was Addy's aphrodisiac.

But in order for her to win her mate completely, she was going to have to make a temporary sacrifice.

"Where did you apply?" Addy asked.

"A few of the shops. I just want to get in somewhere." Cora smiled. She looked relaxed.

There was something different about her. Addy couldn't put her finger on it, but she was happy to see Cora smiling and even walking down the street.

"I want to take you somewhere," Addy admitted. "Do you have time?"

"Yes. I'm done filling out job applications." Cora giggled. She tossed her dark hair over her shoulder, a wicked gleam entering her eye.

The scent of her arousal met Addy's nose. She unconsciously licked her lips, drawing Cora's attention to them.

Cora's voice grew husky. "What do you have in mind?"

Addy blinked. Her mate thought she wanted to

do something sexual. She turned away and checked the streets, hiding her smirk.

She would put her plan into place now.

"It's a surprise." Addy threw the car in drive and maneuvered into the light traffic. There were plenty of people out and about in town enjoying the weather. "But I promise you will love it."

"What is it?" Cora wiggled in her seat with a wide grin on her face.

Addy's heart stuttered at how beautiful her mate was. How did she get so lucky to be blessed by the fates with a woman like Cora?

"We'll be there in a few minutes." Addy guided the car to a place she knew Cora would feel at home in.

The scent of her mate's arousal was driving her insane. Addy swallowed hard, trying to control the animalistic urges. Her gums burned from her fangs pressing against them.

She parked the car in an empty spot on the road in front of their destination.

Turning the car off, she inhaled sharply, taking one last long draw of Cora's sweet smell.

"Come on." Addy motioned for them to exit. She stepped out of the car and rounded the side to meet Cora at her door.

"Rapture?" Cora raised her perfectly sculpted eyebrows. "What kind of place is this?"

Addy glanced at the storefront and tried to see it as Cora did. The windows were covered in dark lace curtains, and a neon light sign in the corner advertised a psychic medium.

Addy pointed to the smaller sign hanging in the window.

Old World Witchery.

Cora's eyes lit up. She grinned and dashed toward the door. Addy chuckled and followed behind her. They entered and were met with the calming fragrance of night air under a full moon.

Addy wasn't sure how Kira could bottle a scent as wonderful as that.

"Oh my." Cora turned around, taking it all in. There were rows of shelves with anything a witch would need. Herbs, homemade oils, candles, books, and exclusive witch wares. It was popular amongst real witches and tourists. "Who owns this shop?"

"My cousin, Kira," Addy announced proudly.

"May I help you—Oh, Addy!" Kira gasped. Her cousin strode forward, looking every part of a witch. Her dark-brown hair hung in waves down her back, a tank top showcasing the tattoos on her arms. They shared a brief hug, her gaze landing on Cora when they separated.

Kira and Addy were extremely distant cousins. Their grandmothers were first cousins. One a witch and one a shifter. They had grown up close, always honoring their family connection.

"Who's your friend?" Kira jerked her head toward Cora.

"Kira, this is Cora. Cora, Kira." Addy made quick introductions. She watched them size each other up without a word.

"So you're the newcomer," Kira murmured.

"I am."

Addy glanced between them as if she were watching a tennis match. She wasn't sure what was going on, but the two women didn't say a word.

"That's some power you're wielding," Kira said.

Addy stiffened. She didn't feel Cora's energy, leading her to believe that her mate was suppressing it as she always did.

"How are you doing it?" Kira asked.

"Wait. What's going on?" Addy asked. She wasn't sure if they were having some kind of witch show off, but she needed to know what the hell they were talking about.

Kira was a member of the local coven, the

White Lotus. It was a small coven, but the members were strong. The coven was historic, having been founded back in the early nineteenth century.

"She knows what I'm talking about." Kira broke the stare and glanced at Addy. She motioned for them to follow her. "For this conversation, we are going to need some tea."

"Got anything stronger?" Cora asked, trailing behind Kira.

"Hell yeah."

Addy stood frozen, lost about what just happened in front of her.

"Are you coming, wolf?" Kira called out.

Addy jerked as if being brought out of a trance. She scurried behind them, not wanting to be left behind.

Chapter Twelve

"Thank you." Cora took the glass handed to her.

Kira offered a tight smile, sitting across the table from her and Addy.

Kira had invited them in the back room of her shop. Cora had known the second Kira looked at her, that she had known about the ward.

Only witches would have sensed it.

And from the looks of it, Kira was no shabby witch.

Addy had settled into a seat next to her and took her cousin up on a stiff drink.

"So, tell me. How and why is there a ward surrounding my town?" Kira didn't hold any punches.

Cora took a sip of her vodka tonic. Apparently, the witch kept a nicely stocked bar for off-hours company.

"A what?" Addy sputtered, putting her glass down.

Cora sheepishly glanced at her. She hadn't had a chance to even share this with Addy yet, but it appeared as if she would be now.

"A ward. A protection spell that is blanketing the entire town," Kira repeated. She leaned back in her chair with an impressed look. "We sensed it the second it went up. We just couldn't figure out who was powerful enough to pull it off. The energy it would take to maintain something this large would take an entire coven."

Cora sensed Addy's eyes on her. Cora took another sip of her drink then set it down on the table.

"Yes, it was me," she admitted. Cora sat back and released a sigh. "I had to do it. This was one of the only ways I felt that I could try to protect everyone here."

Kira regarded her with admiration in her eyes.

She looked over at Addy who gave her a nod as if sensing what Cora wanted to ask out loud.

Could she trust Kira and the local coven.

"It's all right. You can trust her and the White Lotus." Addy reached out a hand and covered Cora's. "They can help. You don't have to do this alone."

"A friend of Addy's is a friend of mine, but it would seem you two are more than friends." Kira grinned and leaned her elbows on the table.

"Yes, we are more than friends." Cora squeezed Addy's hand. She held her gaze for a moment longer then tore it away. She glanced over at Kira and smiled. "My knowing has awakened for Addy."

"And my wolf has identified her as my mate."

"Aww…Addy. I'm so happy for the both of you." Kira sighed.

"But to get back to why I had to put up the ward, I am in danger, and so is Howling Valley." Cora released Addy's hand and shared her story with Kira.

The witch's eyes grew round as she got to the details of Derwin wanting to claim her for her powers. Addy's low growls interrupted her here and there, but for the most part, she remained silent, allowing Cora to tell the tale.

"Wait, Derwin Cross. From Oceana?" Kira gasped.

Cora picked up her drink and gulped down the

rest of it. This couldn't be good. She had only mentioned him by first name.

"Yeah," she replied wearily. "How did you know you know his name?"

"We've heard that there was a coven who went dark. The news has been all over the message boards."

Kira stood and snagged her tablet from the counter where she'd made their drinks.

Cora knew of what she spoke. The Divinity was an online message board website that allowed witches from far and wide to communicate.

If news had reached the message boards, Derwin didn't care who knew what he was doing.

That would mean he was getting reckless.

Cora took the tablet from Kira and scanned the site. There were many discussions regarding her former town and coven. Addy leaned in close, wrapping an arm around her waist. She didn't say a word but offered her support.

Cora clicked on each and every discussion of her coven. From what she read, things didn't look good for Oasis Moon. Her beloved coven was in ruins, falling into dark magic.

"I just wish I knew if my parents made it out of Oceana," Cora murmured. She hadn't dared log in to the message boards once she'd left for fear she would have been tracked.

"It's been said he's looking for something that was of great value for him. The man is sick, and we thought a relic of some sort." Kira paused. Her eyes widened as she realized what Derwin was searching for. "He's after you."

Cora swallowed hard and turned away. "I didn't want to have anything to do with him. I can't turn dark. That is not my destiny."

"He won't touch you," Addy vowed. "My pack won't let that happen."

"Nor will the White Lotus. We will stand beside you. That crazed lunatic must be stopped," Kira said fiercely.

"I can't ask that of you. This is my fight—"

"You are the mate of my cousin," Kira interjected. "That makes you family, and family stands with each other."

"But—"

"It's pointless to argue with her. She's more stubborn than I am," Addy added. She pulled Cora in close and plopped a kiss to her cheek. "I told you, Howling Valley will be fine. Derwin may try to step a foot in our town, that doesn't mean he will leave with it."

Cora giggled. She closed her eyes and briefly imagined Derwin hobbling away from this small town. The goddess above knew what she was doing when she put this town in Cora's path.

Addy glanced over at Kira who was clearing the table of their empty glasses.

"Cuz, did I see a help sign in the window?"

"You sure did." Kira placed the glasses in the small sink then turned around. "Know anyone looking for a job?"

Addy pointed to Cora. Cora's cheeks heated.

"I couldn't." She shook her head. She thought about the quaint little shop, and her heart warmed. It was her type of store that she would spend all of her time in. There were so many books that she could browse through and trinkets along with anything she would need for simple spells. Her gaze hadn't missed the odd door they'd passed on the way to the back. A hint of magic could be sensed.

Cora was sure it led to a special area that was for private clients only.

Someone of the magical sort like herself.

"Why not? You're new to town, I'm sure you need a way to earn money. I'm a shop owner who needs someone to help run my store. I pay well." Kira sat in front of her. She looked her up and down. "And with the size of the ward surrounding us, I already know you are well qualified."

Cora glanced at Addy who was grinning ear to ear.

"What do you have to lose?" Addy chuckled. "I saw the way your eyes lit up when you walked across the threshold. You are in love with Rapture."

Cora felt herself give in. Her lips lifted up in the corner. "Okay, if you're sure you think I'm fit to help with your shop, then I'd love to apply." She sat up taller in her chair.

"On one condition." Kira's eyes got that same mischievous gleam in them that Addy got.

These two were definitely related.

"Oh?"

"You must come to the next coven meeting, and just to let you in on a little hint, I'm not taking no for an answer." Kira offered her a wide smile.

"I…uh…okay. Yes, I'd love to come meet with your coven."

"Then you're hired." Kira held out her hand.

Cora took it in a firm grip.

"How's Monday for your start day?" Kira asked.

"Monday will be fine."

They stood from the table and walked back

through the shop. Kira showed her around, trailing behind them on the way outside.

"Y'all have a great weekend," Kira shouted to them as they got in the car. She remained by the door.

Cora and Addy waved, and Addy guided the car into traffic.

Excitement filled Cora. She was slowly making Howling Valley a home. She was so happy she was ready to burst, but at the back of her mind, she couldn't stop thinking about what she had read on the message boards.

It all led to what she already knew. Derwin was dangerous. He was hunting her, and her senses were shouting that it was only a matter of time until he showed himself.

But would the Nightstar Pack and the White Lotus be enough to help her? In the months since she'd left Oceana, she didn't know all that Derwin had been involved in.

From the message boards, she'd gathered he had let his true nature out. He had turned to the dark side and he was testing and breaking every law covens were to uphold.

That meant he was beyond dangerous.

He must be stopped.

Cora would have to do it. No matter the cost, she would be willing to pay the price to protect the innocents. The more people she got to know in Howling Valley, the more she came to care for this town.

If she had to sacrifice herself to keep this town in one piece, she wouldn't hesitate to do it.

* * *

"Hey, ladies." Malissa grinned as she hopped into the backseat of Addy's car. They were heading over to Grove Hill for their pack's Waxing Moon celebration.

"Hello," Cora said.

"What's up with the bag?" Addy glanced in the review mirror, her gaze landing on her friend's bag.

"Well, just in case I meet a nice wolf who wants to take me home, this is my 'spend a night' bag." Malissa grinned.

Addy rolled her eyes at Malissa. She was always prepared for anything.

Cora and Malissa fell into a light conversation while Addy drove.

Addy anticipated they would have a ton of fun

today. She and Malissa had gone to a few of their Waxing Moon celebrations and had a ball.

It was a large party with a carnival. Their pack would invite wolves from all over. Once the moon rose and the night fell, after the pack run, they held a Treasure Hunt.

Addy had to press her wolf down at the thought of participating in the hunt with Cora.

The Treasure Hunt was an activity where wolves could give in to their carnal needs. They were animals with high sexual appetites. Sex was not something that should be hidden but celebrated.

Addy drove them toward out of town. She thought about the ward Cora had placed over Howling Valley. As she glanced around, she didn't see anything out of the ordinary. She was still amazed at the power it must take for Cora to keep it in place.

She'd seen her mate's work in the forest, but that was a much smaller area for her to hide.

Cora was currently protecting an entire town that housed a few thousand people.

She sat in the front seat of Addy's sedan and didn't look as if she were doing anything at all. That was some power. From what Kira had shared, it would take her entire coven, if not more witches and warlocks to be able to construct something Cora had done in a matter of minutes.

They headed along the highway, coming up on the edge of town. Addy still didn't see anything that would signify a protection dome surrounding it. Her gaze landed on a familiar sign sitting on the side of the road.

Now leaving Howling Valley.

The second they drove past it, a chill passed through Addy. Her gaze connected with Malissa's in the mirror.

"What the hell was that?" Malissa asked. She looked around at herself. "Did anyone else feel that?"

"Feel what?" Cora turned her innocent eyes to Addy, then turned back around to Malissa.

Addy caught the message in her eyes.

Don't say a word.

Addy knew her mate was uneasy with so many people knowing her story. But for now, everyone who was in a position to help her had been brought up to speed on what could happen. Addy was extremely pleased her cousin wanted to take Cora under her wing and introduce her to the coven.

"What are you talking about?" Addy asked,

trying to act as if she didn't sense it. That had to be the effect of them driving through the ward.

"You felt it, too. I could tell." Malissa shivered again. She brushed her hair from her face and pressed her nose to the window. "I'm not crazy. I know I felt something."

Cora remained silent about what they had just gone through.

"How long before we get there?" Cora asked.

Addy glanced down at the clock on the car's dashboard screen. Grove Hill wasn't that far. It was right down the road, should only take them about twenty minutes.

"Not long."

"Have you come to this celebration before?" Cora asked.

Addy nodded. "Yeah. There will be lots of people there. All kinds of shifters will be there, too. The hunt is a popular event."

"I keep hearing you two mention a Treasure Hunt." Cora glanced at both Addy and Malissa. "What is that?"

"I'll let you explain, bestie." Malissa snorted.

"It's a game shifters play that is for adults only." Addy grinned. She looked over at Cora, tossing her a wink before she returned her eyes to the road.

"The targets, or the 'treasure', is released into the wild. They are given a head start to go off and hide. Once time is up, then the hunters are sent out to capture their treasure."

"Oh, but what if you don't have anyone to be paired with?" Cora asked.

"That's what the festivities beforehand are for. I'll use myself as an example. I'm going single, but I'm definitely open for someone to hang with." Malissa wagged her eyebrows. "If I hit it off with someone, then I can either be the treasure or the hunter."

"Sounds fun. So, like hide and seek," Cora asked.

"Bingo," Addy replied. Her gaze flicked to Malissa's in the rearview mirror.

A giggle escaped them until they were both laughing.

"What is so funny?" Cora narrowed her gaze on Addy. "Wait a minute. What happens when the one who is the treasure is caught by the hunter?"

"Let's just say the hunter gets to fully enjoy everything about their prize."

Chapter Thirteen

Cora blew out a nervous breath. The wolves hosting the event in Grove Hill sure knew how to throw a party. There was a fair with plenty of good food, drinks, and activities to keep everyone occupied.

Nighttime had fallen, and she knew that the Treasure Hunt would soon be starting. Being under the moon, with Addy so close, was awakening her knowing.

Cora scooted closer to Addy who was talking with another wolf from Grove Hill. He was a nice guy and apparently knew Addy's elder brother.

Cora's heart raced as she watched Addy smile at the guy. She didn't hear a word they were saying, she was too focused on how good Addy looked. Her long auburn hair was plaited in a sloppy braid that rested on her shoulders. Her tank top highlighted her smooth skin that Cora wanted to explore.

They were seated along a grassy knoll. Addy had brought them over to it to enjoy their corn dogs and funnel cakes. It had been the perfect date. Malissa had left them about an hour ago. She had met up with someone she knew and ditched Addy and Cora, stating she was done being the third wheel.

"I'll tell him I saw you." Addy laughed.

The wolf gave her a wave and smiled at Cora before walking away.

Addy turned to Cora, glancing at the paper plates on the grass that Cora had put in a neat pile. "Did you want anything else?"

Cora shook her head. Food wasn't on her mind. Her gaze dropped down to Addy's plump lips, and she bit back a groan. She remembered what it was like to feel those lips pressing along her body.

It had been too long since she had been gifted the pleasure of Addy's tongue.

Cora pushed up from her spot and promptly straddled Addy's lap. She wrapped her arms around her mate's neck. Addy's golden eyes watched her.

"I take it you are wanting something else,"

Addy murmured. Her nostrils flared. "Hmmm...I can scent you, my love."

"I'm not surprised," Cora admitted. Her body was craving Addy's touch. Her core was drenched with need. She bent down, covering Addy's lips with hers.

A moan erupted from Cora. Addy's lips were just as soft as she remembered. She slipped her tongue into Addy's mouth, stroking her tongue with hers. Cora rocked her pelvis against Addy's stomach.

She was in desperate need of release. She didn't care who was around them. The festivities of the night had already begun. Cora had already witnessed a few couples sneaking away.

Addy's hands cupped her ass, holding her close. Their kiss grew deeper. Cora couldn't get close enough to Addy.

Cora's breasts grew heavy.

There would be no time for the hunt; she wanted to drag Addy into a small corner of the woods and have her way with her.

"Cora..." Addy tore her lips from her and offered Cora her sexy grin.

Cora's heart was pounding against her chest. Her core pulsed with need.

"The hunt shall be waiting soon."

"I don't want to wait." Cora pouted. She pressed her breasts against Addy's. Her nipples had pebbled into hard little buds. The clothing covering her body was becoming an irritant. She wanted them gone.

Addy's hand skated along her back and disappeared underneath her shirt. Her warm hands sent a shiver down Cora's spine.

"But you must," Addy whispered.

"Why?" Cora leaned forward and nipped Addy's bottom lip. It was as if she had no control over her body. She glanced down and saw Addy's nipples were pushing against her tank.

Cora grew bold and cupped the full mound. A growl vibrated from Addy. Cora flicked her gaze to Addy's, finding her eyes locked on her.

Addy reached up, threading her fingers into Cora's long dark tresses. She held Cora still, staring into her eyes.

Her wolf was near the surface.

Excitement filled Cora.

"Because we're going to participate in the hunt." Bell chimes ringing interrupted Addy. It was the signal the hunt was about to begin.

Cora's core clenched at the thought of being chased by Addy.

A wolfish grin appeared on Addy's face. "You better run fast, my witch. Because when I catch you, I'm claiming you in every way known to wolves."

"You are just so sure you will catch me?" Cora lifted her eyebrows. She couldn't help but tease her wolf.

Addy growled, narrowing her gaze on Cora.

"I will, witch." She reached up and slid her hand along Cora's neck, resting it on the juncture between her neck and shoulder. "Right here, I will put my mark."

A whimper escaped Cora. Addy's warm hand caressed the skin that was so sensitive at the moment.

"You belong to me. Tonight, I will claim you. Sealing the bond between us with one bite."

Cora took in the others who were deemed to be the 'treasure'. Women and men waited at the starting point. They had been given clear instructions. They were to run through the forest since they were the prey and hide.

"The end of the hunt will be marked by sunshine or capture," a deep voice boomed.

Cora blinked and glanced over to where the man was. Elder members of their local pack stood with him. The hunt was apparently a big event that many came to Grove Hill to participate in.

Cora saw Malissa standing amongst the group. She winked at Cora before turning away.

Looked like she did find a partner for the night.

The moon was high and was shining down brightly on them. Cora was trying to devise a plan. She didn't want Addy to catch her immediately. If she were to shift into her animal to chase after Cora, she would catch her quickly. There was no way Cora could outrun a large wolf.

But she could outsmart her.

Cora would use her magic.

Anticipation grew inside her at the memory of Addy's words.

'You better run fast, my witch. Because when I catch you, I'm claiming you in every way known to wolves.'

Cora couldn't wait for Addy to find her, but she wasn't going to make it easy on her. A giggle escaped her.

Why was she fighting what she knew was meant to be?

She and Addy belonged together, and no matter what, the goddess above never made a mistake.

Cora was going to have to put the anxiety of losing Addy aside and bind herself to the wolf. She could not live her life in fear.

She would take back her life and what was meant for her.

Cora glanced around, ready for the signal for them to run. They would have a fifteen-minute head start.

That was plenty of time for Cora to put some distance between them.

"The Treasure Hunt is an annual tradition, practiced for centuries," the emcee boasted. He stood on a platform; his voice boomed. Excitement filled the atmosphere. "Under this moon, give in to your carnal desires. Claim or be claimed."

Cheers and whistles sounded. The crowd was growing rowdier as the night went on. A howl echoed through the air. A couple of wolves returned the call.

Cora's pulse pounded in her ears.

She turned and faced the forest, waiting for the signal.

Bells sounded.

It was time.

Cora took off running into the dark thicket of trees. Footsteps sounded around her. Flashes of some of the other prey running in the woods met her. Her breaths were coming fast. It had been a while since she'd just run.

She had to focus.

Keep her eyes forward; she needed to find a good spot to hide.

Cora skidded to a halt.

What was she doing?

She was a witch.

Her powers would help her.

With a grin, she skipped along, searching for the perfect place for her to rest, all the while touching the tree trunks to leave her mark. The woods were growing darker, but the moon was acting as a guide for her.

Cora followed it for a little before the bells sounded again. The hunters would be released.

Cora spun around and glanced in the direction Addy would be.

Wolves were extremely fast sprinters, and it was only a matter of time until Addy reached the area Cora was in.

She was sure she had left enough of her scent along the way for Addy to find her.

A large bolder came into view, and Cora rushed over to it. She climbed up along the rock and took a seat. She would wait, but only with the assistance of her magic.

She lifted her hand and whispered words of an invisibility spell.

Howls went up in the distance. The wolves were on the hunt.

Cora's heart raced. She couldn't wait for Addy to come her way. She wondered if Addy would be in her wolf or human form.

Just thinking of her soul mate searching for her, had her body growing warm. There was something about being hunted down by Addy that turned her on.

Something trampled through the forest at a distance. Cora focused on the direction of the noise.

The animal continued on.

But it wasn't Addy.

Cora listened closely as the sounds of the woods grew louder. The hunters were out in full force, looking for their treasure.

A growl sounded close.

Cora froze.

It was familiar.

Cora smiled and slid down from her perch.

Addy wouldn't be able to see her, thanks to her spell. She stood still and waited for the beast to come through the brush. Golden eyes were visible, peeking through the leaves of the bushes directly across from Cora.

Addy.

Small waves of desire rushed through her body. Her nipples grew into tight buds, achingly pushing against the soft material of her shirt.

It had been a few days since her last orgasm, and she was craving one. She needed Addy to help ease the ache between her legs.

Her wolf would scent her arousal and know she was slick and ready for her.

The wolf scanned the area, not seeing her. Addy inhaled sharply, apparently having smelled Cora.

Cora took a step back, her pulse pounding in her ears. The rushing of her blood was deafening. With a giggle, Cora ran.

Addy howled.

Cora took off running, no longer caring to remain quiet. She wanted Addy to be able to find her.

But would Addy be able to catch her if she couldn't see her?

Footsteps pounded the ground behind her. Cora dashed around a tree and headed toward a clearing.

Addy was gaining on her.

Cora broke through the clearing just as a large fur-covered body slammed into her. Cora's fall was softened by a thick grass. She tumbled over onto her back and found herself gazing into familiar amber eyes.

Cora released the spell.

"How the hell did you catch me?" she muttered.

The wolf responded with a wide grin. She leaned down and licked Cora's face.

"Stop." Cora laughed. "Give me my Addy."

The animal whined, nuzzling the side of her neck with her snout. Her large claws were resting on the ground next to Cora.

She took the time to study Addy in her wolf form. She was a magnificent beast. Even in the moonlight she could tell how beautiful her animal was.

"Come on," Cora purred. She reached up and ran a hand through her fur. "Give me Addy."

The wolf stared her down before snorting. The air between them shimmered as the shift overtook her. Within seconds, a very naked Addy was poised over Cora. Her long red hair hung down, creating a curtain for them.

"Even with your spells, I'd find you," Addy murmured. She bent down and pressed her lips against Cora's. The kiss was intense, hot and full of tongue.

Addy dominated the kiss, her tongue slipping past Cora's lips. Their tongues dueled together in an age-old dance. Cora reached up and cupped Addy's full breast. Her nipples were drawn into tight buds. She pinched the nipple, eliciting a groan from Addy.

"There are too many clothes between us," Addy groused.

Before Cora had a chance to protest, Addy hands shifted slightly. She ripped Cora's shirt straight down the middle.

A gasp escaped Cora.

Next went her bra, and her skirt didn't fare any better.

Cora's body arched off the ground as Addy pulled the material from her, leaving her in nothing but her panties and sandals.

"Addy," Cora groaned. Goosebumps lined her arms from the slight chill of the night. Even thought it was warm throughout the day, at night, the temperature dropped.

Cora's nipples were painfully erect. Addy's head swooped down, capturing one of her nipples in her mouth. She moaned, threading her finger into Addy's hair, holding her in place.

Addy's hot mouth felt wonderful on her breasts.

Addy released the first one, moving over to the other. Cora sighed, glancing down and watching Addy take her time suckling her breasts. She released it and glanced up at Cora.

"Mine." Addy's voice deepened to a growl.

"Yes, yours," Cora agreed.

Addy trailed her lips farther down Cora's body. She left openmouthed kisses along the way.

She reached Cora's center, and with a growl, ripped the thin material from Cora's body. Her hands gripped Cora's knees and jerked them apart, spreading her wide open.

Cora's heart raced, watching Addy settle on the ground with her face between her legs.

"Please," Cora begged.

"What do you want, my love?" Addy asked. She pressed a kiss to Cora's inner thigh.

"I want your mouth on me," Cora cried out.

She could barely keep her body still. The plush grass underneath her was a thick, soft bed.

"Where?" Addy slid her tongue along Cora's thigh toward her pussy. She stopped right at the crease of her thigh and pelvis. Her sharp fangs lightly pinched Cora's skin.

"My pussy," Cora gasped. Her eyes rolled in the back of her head the second Addy's tongue slid along her slit. She widened her legs to ensure Addy would have full access to her.

Addy moaned, her tongue dipping into Cora's wet heat. She took her time tasting Cora. Her talented tongue slid up to tease her swollen clit.

"Yes," Cora hissed.

Addy suckled her clit, and Cora's back arched up off the ground.

If something was going to kill her, this would be the best way to go.

Addy's hands rested on the back of her legs while they kept Cora open for her.

Cora's body trembled, the sensations in her body increasing. She trembled fiercely with every suck and flick of Addy's tongue.

Her body was on fire.

A low growl emanated from Addy, and she

continued to feast on Cora. It wasn't a threatening sound but one of intense passion.

Cora's eyes fluttered shut, and she turned her pleasure completely over to Addy.

This was her other half.

What was she thinking of, trying not to seal the bond between the two of them? Goddess only knew how the sex would be once they completed their mating.

Cora's arousal coated her thighs. It poured from her. Addy pushed two fingers inside her. Cora lifted her hips to meet Addy's hand as she slowly thrust them in and out of her slick core. Her tongue teased Cora's clit.

The sound of something crashing through the woods came across the clearing.

Cora was teetering close to her orgasm. She could feel it creeping toward her.

Desperately, Cora reached out to hold on to something. She gripped the grass tight, anchoring herself. Her hips moved in rhythm with Addy's fingers.

A deep groan sounded near them.

Cora's eyes flashed open. The moon's rays shined down on their little alcove, giving her just enough light to see.

Her gaze landed on two males in the throes of passion. A dark-haired male was braced over a blond. They were naked, sharing a deep, passionate kiss.

It would seem another hunter had found his treasure.

Cora was unable to look away.

The dark-haired male flipped the blond over onto his hands and knees while kneeling behind him. He gripped his long cock and thrust it inside his lover.

Cora's breath caught in her throat.

She had never considered the life of voyeurism before, but at the moment, she was all about watching while getting her pussy eaten out by her own mate.

Their grunts and groans echoed through the air.

Addy increased the pressure on her clit. Cora cried out, her one free hand landing on the back of Addy's head. She threaded her fingers through the dark-auburn locks, holding her in place. Her fingers pounded into Cora's slick opening, while she flicked Cora's clit with her tongue.

Cora continued to watch the dark-haired male

fuck his mate hard. His hips pistoned faster as the blond cried out in ecstasy.

"Goddess above," Cora sobbed. The tremors coursing through her body took over her.

Addy nipped her swollen nub with her fang, sending Cora over the edge.

Her body detonated.

A scream erupted from her lips. An electric current rushed through her body. She rode the waves of her climax.

Cora flopped back down onto the ground, her body left trembling from the expanse of energy. She closed her eyes, trying to catch her breath.

Addy lifted her head from Cora's center. She crawled over Cora and braced herself above her.

Her lips curled back, revealing her sharp fangs. Her chest rumbled, while her eyes appeared to glow even brighter.

"Mine."

Chapter Fourteen

"Claim me," Cora whispered. She turned her head, exposing her neck fully to Addy.

The taste of Cora's sweet nectar still lingered on Addy's tongue. Her gaze flicked over to the couple across the clearing before returning to Cora.

"From the moment I scented you, I knew you belonged to me," Addy admitted. She bent her head down and nuzzled Cora's neck. She licked the column, taking in the taste of her skin.

Cora's jugular pulsed, her heart rate increasing.

The taste and scent of Cora was embedded into Addy's senses. She would always recognize her mate.

Having Cora reach her climax on her tongue always had her painfully aroused. She had denied herself the pleasure of fucking Cora, but no longer. Tonight, they were going all the way.

"I knew it, too, but I didn't want to believe that it could be possible to find you," Cora whispered. She reached up and cupped Addy's face.

Addy lowered her face to Cora. She kissed her, slow and deep. Addy wanted to cherish this time between them.

Cora's tongue was confidently stroking hers. Addy could stay here forever kissing her, but for now, she had more important matters at hand. Her core was slick, and her clit was swollen, needing release.

Addy tore her mouth from Cora's, staring down at her.

"Open your legs, my darling," Addy murmured. She braced herself on one hand, while the other one skated along Cora's voluminous breasts. Her hand molded to one mound, pinching her nipple.

Cora's gasp filled her ears. Her attention was fully on her mate lying underneath her. The sounds of the two males across the way grew louder.

Had she not been about to claim her mate, she would have watched along with Cora.

But at the moment, she had something else that was a little more pressing.

Cora's legs widened, allowing Addy to maneuver herself over Cora. She straddled her, lowering her dripping core onto Cora's.

Addy groaned, reaching between them to part her folds. The action allowed her sensitive clit to rest on Cora's.

"Yes," Cora hissed, her hands coming to rest on Addy's waist. She rotated her hips, creating friction between them.

She held Cora's gaze as they moved together.

Addy pressed her center to Cora's. Their moans were growing louder. Their movements increased. Addy's gums burned and stretched as her fangs descended.

Cora guided her closer, to allow her breasts to sway in front of her ace. She reached up and captured one of Addy's breasts with her mouth. She suckled the breast as if her life depended upon it.

A strong tug could be felt clear down to her pussy.

Addy's thighs were coated in their juices.

A possessiveness overcame Addy. Her gaze latched on to Cora's shoulder.

Mine.

The one word echoed in her head.

She had to claim Cora so she would only belong

to her.

Cora released her breasts, her head falling back to the ground. Her eyelashes fluttered against her creamy skin, her expression one of pure ecstasy.

Addy's body trembled with an electric current flowing through her.

Cora's hands slipped down to Addy's ass, encouraging their quick motions.

"Mine." This time the word slipped from her mouth. Her wolf was pacing, waiting for the perfect moment.

"Then make me yours," Cora whispered, turning her head away to expose the column of her neck.

A red haze overcame Addy's vision.

Her animal pushed her forward. Planting open-mouthed kisses along Cora's neck, she breathed in her scent and that of her arousal.

The air grew thick around them. Her attention was only on her mate beneath her, as if they were the only two people in the world.

Nothing existed at the moment except for them.

She opened her mouth wide, her fangs sinking down into the meat of Cora's shoulder. Her body shuddered with the copper taste of Cora's blood exploding on her tongue.

Cora jerked in response, her body growing tense, and she screamed through her orgasm. A surge of energy whipped through the atmosphere around them.

Addy's climax slammed into her. She released her mate and threw her head back, bellowing her release.

Her wolf howled in response.

They had finally claimed their mate.

Their bodies stilled, their legs tangled together. Cora flopped back down on the soft grass underneath her, eyes closed, chest rising and falling fast.

Addy's wolf was finally satisfied.

Addy's gaze moved to Cora's shoulder. She leaned down and licked the wound to stop the flow of blood.

Something was different about her. She could feel a tether around her heart. A smile graced her lips.

It would seem Cora had allowed her goddess to bind them together.

Her witch had claimed her, too.

It was a different feeling, but one that Addy would be proud to experience. There was now a link between them, and from what she knew of witches, it was forever.

Addy liked it.

Knowing her mate wanted to spend forever with her, stroked her ego.

She moved Cora's hair to fully see her shoulder, and pride filled her that her woman's skin was marred with her mark.

It would heal.

But the mark of a wolf's claiming would always remain.

In the eyes of the shifters and witches, they were officially mated.

Cora's shoulder was sore, but it would heal. She was beyond happy she and Addy had taken the final step and mated.

Inside her chest, her knowing was now settled and quiet.

She turned into Addy's arms and pressed a chaste kiss to her lips. They were still in their little clearing, now alone. The two males had moved on. The sounds of the forest let them know that there were others still out there. Moans, growls, and shouts of ecstasy could be easily heard, but Cora didn't care.

Right now, it was her and the other half of her soul, lying together underneath the moon and the magnificent dark sky.

The moment she was hit with her second orgasm before Addy bit her, she allowed her knowing to take over. The energy that flowed from her, bound Addy to her.

She would never let her wolf go. No one would separate them. Cora was willing to fight to the death to ensure that her soul mate remained unharmed.

There was no more hiding what she was. Howling Valley was going to be her home, and no one was going to take her from it.

Cora closed her eyes briefly and allowed the shields she had kept in place to hide her magic fall.

Addy's eyes immediately opened. "What are you doing?"

"I'm done with hiding," Cora murmured. She breathed a sigh of relief. It was like a weight was lifted from her shoulders. She was going to maintain the wards over Howling Valley to protect the town she had come to love.

But for her, she was who she was.

Cora Latimer, a powerful witch who was ready to reveal all that she was.

"Are you sure?"

"I'm certain." Cora looked to the moon that was sitting high. The goddess would protect them.

Addy pulled her closer in her embrace. Their soft breasts were crushed between them, but Cora would not complain. Her breath caught in her throat at the feeling of Addy's hard nipples brushing hers.

"So I take it this means that we are going to move me into your home now?" Cora chuckled.

"Damn right, we are," Addy muttered. She ran a hand lazily down Cora's naked back.

A shiver rippled through Cora at the light touch.

"We will not be apart from each other any longer," Addy said.

Cora grinned at the possessiveness in her mate's voice. Addy was a true wolf.

Headstrong.

Stubborn.

Cora loved it.

A sigh escaped her. She studied Addy's features and knew without a doubt she was in love with this woman.

Why did I try to fight it?

Never again.

She leaned over and pressed a kiss to the column of Addy's neck. Her golden eyes were locked on Cora. She lifted her head and nipped Addy's bottom lip which elicited a low rumble of a growl from her wolf.

Cora grinned. She pushed herself up and moved over Addy. Her wolf immediately rolled onto her back, silently giving Cora control.

In all of the times they had been intimate before, she had never got to return a certain favor to Addy.

Cora took advantage and trailed kisses from Addy's neck down. She took her time moving lower down to Addy's perky breasts. She captured one and slowly tasted both of them. She drew little circles around Addy's nipple with her tongue.

Addy's body trembled. She didn't say a word but allowed Cora to feast on her breasts. She grasped the thick grass beneath her.

Cora knew the wolf in Addy would demand she control everything, but she was giving it to Cora. Her heart skipped a beat at the notion.

They had all night.

This Treasure Hunt was all about carnal pleasures.

Cora had to hand it to the wolves, it was a fabulous idea.

A night dedicated to pleasure.

Cora continued on her travels, kissing and licking Addy's body as she moved lower. She finally reached her destination. Addy widened her legs, allowing Cora to come face to face with her center.

The scent of Addy's arousal greeted her.

Even in the low light, Cora could make out Addy's perfect pussy. Her swollen clit was exposed. Her labia glistened with her wetness.

Cora's fingers connected with the swollen bud. She teased Addy by drawing slow circles on her flesh.

A moan escaped Addy.

Cora licked her lips, witnessing how wet her mate was.

Parting Addy's folds, she leaned forward and captured her clitoris with her lips. Addy's body arched off the ground.

She had been waiting for this moment.

Cora was determined to give her mate multiple orgasms.

They weren't leaving from their little piece of heaven until her mouth was filled with Addy's cream.

Chapter Fifteen

Everything was different. It had been a week since Cora and Addy had mated. Cora was living the high life. She had moved into Addy's house that same weekend.

And, as promised, she had started work at Rapture.

She loved it.

She and Kira had hit it off and were already in talks of how they could make the shop better. With Cora's extensive training in herbs and witchcraft, she had a little more to bring to the table than a regular salesperson.

Cora walked down the street, having taken her lunch at the local coffee shop. The sun was high, and she was truly happy. She sipped on her iced coffee and basked in the sensations coursing through her body.

The only thing that would make her completely happy was if she could see her parents.

Or somehow get word to them that she was safe.

She was going to be meeting with the White Locus this weekend. Kira was adamant that they would stand behind her and help her reach her family.

There was no telling what happened to them. She prayed to the goddess above that Marden hadn't lost all of his marbles and had protected them.

Cora reached the corner of the street and paused. The traffic in town was more than usual, but it could be that it was Friday and people were wanting to enjoy the weather. The weekend was upon them, and their little town bustled with everyone hitting the shops and restaurants.

Cora froze in place.

The hairs on the back of her neck stood to attention.

Someone was watching her.

Ever since she'd removed the shield of her powers, most of the paranormals in town had picked up on what she was. The humans wouldn't notice it.

She was used to the curious glances from those who sensed her power, but this was different.

She took another sip of her coffee and casually glanced round. There were a few humans walking down the sidewalk window browsing. A bear shifter tinkered with his motorcycle parked on the curb, but he wasn't paying her any mind.

Her gaze scanned the other side of the street, and she was met with the intense stare of a tall male figure. He was dressed to blend in with the towns-folk: jeans, casual shoes, and black short-sleeved button-down shirt. His arms were marked with tattoos. His size alone stood out. One would assume he was a bear shifter from his height and build, but Rune was a strong warlock guard from her coven.

Rune had been in cahoots with Derwin. He had served under Brumelda, and the second she'd died, his loyalty was immediately known to be for Derwin.

Cora didn't shy away from his glare. His lips tilted up in a devilish smirk.

Her ward hadn't alerted her to Derwin.

But if Rune was here, Derwin wasn't far behind.

Her heart raced.

She knew this day would come, but she hadn't figured it would be this quick before he had found her.

The pedestrian stoplight turned green, giving her permission to cross the street. Keeping her gaze on Rune, she made her way to the other side. She stopped once she stepped onto the curb and faced him. He was still twenty feet from her.

"Cora Latimer." Rune folded his massive arms in front of his chest. He narrowed his eyes on her.

Before, she would have been frightened to face him down.

Not that he wielded more power than her, but she was afraid of being captured and dragged back to Oceana.

He may be physically stronger than her, but there was no one from Oceana who could match her in power.

"What do you want?" She wasn't going to reveal the surprise of seeing him.

"Don't play dumb, witch," he snarled. A dark mask washed over his face.

He stepped toward her, but she held her ground.

She took another pull from her straw. The iced

coffee was the best she'd had, and it cooled her on this hot day. She casually did this to show him that his presence didn't bother her.

On the inside it did. She had hoped she'd have more time than a witch-warlock battle when Derwin arrived.

But if she truly wanted all of this over with, she'd have to face him sooner or later.

"Where is he?" she asked, lifting an eyebrow. Her wards were holding strong.

"This is a fancy trick you're pulling right now. It proves Derwin was right along." He barked a hefty laugh. "Who would have thought Marden's little sister would be so powerful."

She stiffened at the mention of her brother.

"Oh, that got a reaction. How does it feel to have your own flesh and blood turn on you?" He took another step.

She held her ground as he made his way toward her. She tightened her grip on her almost empty cup.

"Marden will pay for his treachery," she retorted.

"You dear brother has risen in the ranks since you left," Rune stated. He stopped in front of her, trying to intimidate her with his size.

"Back away from me," she warned. Her hand tingled from the energy in her flowing to her fingertips. Brumelda had always warned her to never show her true powers, but today would be a day she would have to disobey her mentor. With Brumelda's death, she had tried to listen to her, but now Cora was going to have to make her mark in the world.

"Or what?" He chuckled and lowered his voice. "Is the little witch going to run to her wolf shifter mate and cry?"

Cora narrowed her gaze and met his head-on. Mentioning her mate brought up her defenses. If he knew about Addy, then he'd been in town long enough to observe her.

"Don't ever mention her," she warned. Her energy grew stronger, wisps floating around her hands. Her cup was long forgotten, falling to the ground.

"You and that little wolf bitch have been playing house. Don't worry, we'll take care of her—"

Cora's hand rose swiftly, a bolt of her magic slamming into Rune. He roared, his body flying back at least fifty feet, landing on the ground.

A red haze came over her.

No one threatened her mate.

Cora stood her ground, ready for his onslaught. The air around her sizzled with an electric current.

"You bitch," Rune growled, pushing up from the ground and facing her.

"Is there a problem?" a voice barked. Heavy footsteps stomped across the street. Low growls echoed in the air.

Cora flicked her gaze to the newcomers. Griffin, Lupe, and Jatix, the pack enforcers, made their way to Cora. Their faces were fierce, their amber eyes burning bright. Cora recognized the look.

Their wolves were close to the surface.

She'd seen the same on Addy's face when her animal was nearing.

"I think you need to leave," Griffin stated.

"This is a free country, I can walk down a sidewalk if I want to," Rune spat.

Cora moved so she could look between the bulking bodies of the enforcers.

Addy had promised her the wolves of her pack would have her back; now there was no doubt they did.

The three of them had appeared to come out of nowhere.

Was it a coincidence?

It possibly could be, but in the back of her mind, she didn't think so.

"Not in this town you don't. This is a shifter's town, and we run this," the one named Jatix responded. His baritone voice was deep and guttural.

"This is between me and Cora." Rune took a step forward.

The three wolves growled. Their bodies almost appeared to grow in size as they prepared to defend her.

"He was just leaving," Cora announced. She shoved through the wolves. She was thankful for their presence, but she knew Rune was going to run to Derwin and share with him what he'd learned.

"Not without you." An unsettling glint appeared in Rune's eyes.

She pushed down the fear that reared inside her. Here in Howling Valley, she was safe.

"You are leaving. Without her." Griffin stepped forward. "She's under the protection of the Night-star Pack, and if you have a problem with that, then you deal with us."

"You wolves are cute. You don't know what the fuck you are dealing with." He tipped his chin toward her. "She's dangerous. Her powers are unmatched by no one. Her coven wants her back."

"I am not property," Cora fumed. She clenched her hands into fists. How dare they? Was he trying to scare the wolves into turning her over to them? As if she would harm anyone in Howling Valley. "If you know my powers are unmatched by anyone, then you are stupid to come here alone."

She stepped forward, unleashing the electric current brimming inside her. A quick intake of breath sounded behind her, but her sights were on Rune.

She would give him a message to take back to Derwin, but first, she needed to do one thing.

Cora focused on him, using her power of compulsion to hold him still.

Derwin had sent him as bait, and Rune was too stupid to realize it.

"What are you doing?" Rune tried to fight the hold she had over him.

She strolled to him, having fun with this.

"Let me go." He stood deathly still, his arms at his sides, his feet planted firmly on the ground. Only his eyes moved, following her movements.

"You were a fool to come here." She reached him, standing mere inches from him. Cora stretched a hand toward his face. "Derwin doesn't care about you. You're nothing but a pawn to him."

Her eyes fluttered shut once her fingers rested on his temple.

She was instantly hit with his memories.

"She is the key," Derwin snapped. He paced back and forth.

They were located in the outskirts of Howling Valley. A couple of vehicles were parked on the edge of the highway. The moon was high, and the nighttime sky was void of any stars. Rune stood with Caton and Leif, other members of the warlock guard.

Derwin paused, staring down the road that led to the town. "Her powers are growing."

"What if she's been masking them this entire time?" Caton asked. He was a warlock with dark skin and long black dreadlocks. "She's been working with Brumelda for years. There's a chance your aunt had taught her to hide her powers."

"There was a reason my aunt took the little bitch under her wing." Derwin turned and faced his guards. "Brumelda has always said Cora was special, but I never understood how special until now. No one should be able to *wield that much power. That ward has been in place for a long time."*

"What do you want us to do?" Rune asked. He glanced in the direction of the town and he wanted to go retrieve the little witch. If what Derwin said was true, she would help them unlock the portal for the dark realm. Excitement filled him. If he was the one to retrieve her, he would be rewarded greatly.

"You men have done great work. I may not be able to cross that fucking ward, but you have brought me great infor-mation. She's taken a mate." He paced once again. He became lost in thought.

Derwin was a powerful warlock, and his plan to tap into the dark magic of the other realm was genius. They would become the most powerful coven in the world. When Derwin ascended his throne as the ruler of this realm, Rune hoped to be appointed to a high-ranking position.

"We will go after her. Bring her to me. If she resists, then we will go after her mate. That will make her come." Derwin stopped in his tracks, disgust on his face. "It matters not that she's mated to that wretched wolf, she will be mine. I will tap into her and bring that power out of her."

"If she's bound herself to that woman, how will you break it? Binding to one's soul mate is forever," Leif said.

"You let me worry about that. We need some leverage on her since her parents have disappeared," Derwin snarled.

"Once we have her, we will perform the Torrent Sacré, and all will be mine."

Rune nodded. He didn't know how Marden had lost his own parents. The warlock would pay for his failures. He was currently held in Oceana's jail waiting for his trial and punishment.

"I will bring her to you." Rune nodded to Derwin. By doing this, he would basically solidify his ranking in Derwin's hierarchy.

Derwin walked to him, stopping in front of him. He studied Rune for a moment before returning the nod.

"Bring her to me, and you will be rewarded greatly once the portal to the Dark Realm is opened."

"Yes, sir." Rune stood to his full height. He would not let himself down. He was a strong warlock and had fought in many battles against many enemies. Cora Latimer was a small woman. She was no match for him.

"But know if you fail…" Derwin let his words fade away. He didn't have to say. The coven leader didn't tolerate failure from his guards.

Rune turned without another word and stalked to the first vehicle. He wouldn't need assistance bringing in one witch. They had scoured the western seaboard looking for her.

Thanks to her dropping her energy shield, they were able to find her swiftly.

He hopped in the car and slammed the door.

Cora blinked, pain exploding in her brain. The sound of the door shutting echoed through her head.

Yelling came from behind her, but she couldn't make the words out. She stumbled away from Rune, disconnecting herself from him. Her knees wobbled, her eyes rolled into the back of her head, and then there was nothing.

Chapter Sixteen

Addy's wolf paced inside her chest. Fear was lodged in her throat as she stared down at her mate. Her beautiful Cora was lying unconscious and pale in their bed.

Reaching over, she brushed Cora's dark hair from her face. Her fingers trailed along her cheek.

"Wake up." Addy leaned down and rested her forehead on Cora's. She breathed in, loving her mate's scent. Fear slowly dissipated. Her mate was here and safe. Addy just prayed she woke up soon.

Her heart had about jumped out of her throat when Griffin had arrived with Cora. The memory of him holding her still form had Addy thinking the worst. She would have never forgiven herself if she had lost her love.

He had shared with her the confrontation with the warlock who had approached Cora. Addy's wolf growled even now thinking of the story.

"I should have been there," she whispered. Addy lifted her head, pressing a soft kiss to Cora's pink lips.

"There was nothing you would have been able to do," Kira's voice came from the doorway.

Addy turned and found her cousin leaning against the doorjamb.

"But I could have been there with her." Addy straightened. It had been a little over twenty-four hours since the event.

According to Griffin, they held the warlock captive, trying to get information from him.

"Your mate was wielding some crazy magic. Once she passed out, the wards went down."

Addy froze. That fear came rushing back. It was stifling. She glanced back at Cora. She was exposed. If that warlock knew where she was, then certainly that Derwin character knew it, too.

"Can you put it back up?" Addy asked, even though she already knew the answer.

Kira shook her head. She walked over to them and stood near the edge of the bed. "I wish I could, but it would take the entire coven to even attempt it, and even then, I can't guarantee it would work." Kira exhaled.

"Why won't she wake up? Our pack healer said there wasn't anything they could find wrong with her." Addy took Cora's hand in hers and held it tightly. She rubbed the back of it with her free one.

"Her body went into overload. From the ward she had constructed, and then it would seem she did a memory walk on the warlock. It's no wonder her body shut down."

"Memory walk?" Addy glanced up at her cousin. They may be distant relatives, but there were still things that Addy didn't know about her cousin's kind. Her focus turned back to Cora. She was amazed every day by what she kept learning about her mate. "Is that even possible?"

"It is very rare. There are some witches who can catch glimpses, but as long as Lupe said she was touching the warlock, I'm willing to bet she was able to see much more."

"Amazing." Addy brought Cora's hand to her lips and pressed a kiss to it. Now if only her love would awaken so she could tell her what she'd seen.

"Is there anything you need?" Kira asked.

Addy shook her head. "Can you awaken her?"

"No, I'm sorry, cuz. That will happen when she

is ready." Kira moved close to Addy and rested her hand on Addy's shoulder. "I'll be out there with your family."

Addy nodded. Kira padded out of the room, leaving Addy alone with her sleeping mate.

This was not how she wanted her family to meet her mate. They had planned have dinner with her parents tomorrow. The second word had reached her parents and siblings that her mate was in trouble, they had arrived at her house to help.

She would have gone insane had it not been for her family.

There wasn't much they could do, but having them here gave her comfort.

From the smells coming from downstairs, her mother had busied herself in the kitchen.

Addy pushed off the bed and walked over to the window. She brushed the curtain to the side and found the enforcers sitting out there.

Jatix and Decker were there for protection.

Addy's gut was shouting that it wasn't going to be enough. If what Kira had said was true about the wards, then Derwin would soon show himself.

She hoped he was ready for a fight, because that was what he was going to get. There was no way he was taking Cora.

Addy would fight him to the death to protect her mate.

She was in love with Cora. Without a doubt. Addy was coming to learn so much about her and that fate had chosen the perfect person for her.

Not that she ever doubted fate. The moment she had heard Cora's voice, she knew she would be the person she would spend all eternity with.

Discovering everything about her just made her want to claim her all over again.

Moving away from the window, she sat back down on the bed. After Griffin had brought Cora to their room, Addy had removed her clothing and gave her a sponge bath as best as she could to rid Cora of the dirt and grime that was on her. She'd dressed her in a cotton nightshirt and covered her up with the blanket.

All throughout the night, Addy had stayed by Cora's side.

Her wolf would not rest or settle until Cora's beautiful blue eyes opened.

"Baby, come back to me," she whispered to Cora. Addy pressed her lips to Cora's delicate ear. She wasn't sure this was going to work, but it was worth a try. "I don't know if you can hear my voice, but if you do, come to me. It's so lonely without you. My sun doesn't shine as bright without you, the air isn't as sweet without the sound of your laugh. I need you. I love you so much."

The room remained silent.

Addy exhaled. She didn't know what else to do. She guessed she would have to learn how to be patient. She lifted her head and found Cora's beautiful blue eyes on her.

"Cora—"

"I love you, too," Cora's husky voice filled her ears.

Addy's heart filled with joy hearing those words. She leaned down and covered Cora's mouth with hers in a hard, bruising kiss.

They separated, breathing heavy.

"Are you all right?" Addy exhaled. She studied Cora's face and didn't see any pain, allowing her to relax slightly.

"I'm fine. I think I just overdid it." Cora grimaced. She attempted to sit up.

Addy jumped out of the way and helped Cora settle back against the pillows.

"How long have I been out?" Cora asked.

"A little over twenty-four hours," Addy replied. Her wolf whined, wanting to be released so she could check on Cora herself. Addy pushed her back. She would have her time later. "Kira said the wards are down."

Cora nodded. "I know."

"Did you truly memory walk?" Addy asked hesitantly. She took her mate's hand in hers, needing to touch her.

"I did, and even though it drained me, I'm so glad I did." Cora's lips turned into a wide grin.

"Why is that?" Addy asked. Worry filled her. This magic trick of Cora's was obviously too much for her. What if she was hurt doing it?

"Because I was able to go into the memories of Rune—"

"You know him? The warlock?" Addy asked.

"Oh, yes. He was a warlock guard for Brumelda, my former priestess. But the minute Derwin took over, he sided with him." Cora leaned back against the pillows and closed her eyes. She inhaled in softly before continuing. "I was able to see his last conversation with Derwin before he came into town. I learned something that gives me hope."

"What is that?" Addy brought Cora's hand to her lips, kissing it softly. She was blown away by how powerful Cora was. If Kira was in awe by the strength of Cora, then it meant her mate was one hell of a witch.

"My parents are alive. They escaped. Apparently, my brother lost them." Cora smiled.

"That's amazing. We can start looking for them." Addy immediately thought of who she could reach out to help look for her mate's parents. Her wolf paced, sensing the importance of what they would need to do.

"But first, we still have to deal with Derwin," Cora whispered, bringing Addy back to the present.

Addy blinked, having already forgotten about the evil warlock. She understood how much this changed everything for her mate. She had thought this Derwin character had her parents, possibly harming them.

"Of course. You know you won't be doing this alone." She squeezed Cora's hand tight. Her wolf whined, wanting to put in her two cents, too.

"I know, and that's why I love you so much. You aren't turning away from me and everything that I have to deal with."

"Never." A growl erupted from Addy. That was her wolf. There was no way in the seven hells she'd ever turn her back on her mate. Their bond was for life, and even in the afterlife. Her wolf was ready to go to war to keep Cora safe.

She may be a schoolteacher, but that didn't take away from the fact that her inner animal could be vicious and protective about the ones she loved.

"He's on his way," Cora announced softly. Her blue eyes did a weird thing where the color almost faded away. She blinked, and immediately it was gone.

"When?" Addy stood from the bed. She had to warn her family and the alpha.

"We have no time." Cora threw the covers off her and moved to the edge of the bed.

"What do you mean? My parents, brother, and sister, along with Kira, are downstairs. Two enforcers are outside. You are safe." Addy rested her hands on her waist as Cora stood. It would be pointless to try to push her back down; her mate was just as stubborn as she was.

"Your sister is pregnant, your brother has a family. They are not to be involved." Cora shook her head and walked over to the closet.

"How much time?" Addy bit out through clenched teeth. She spun around and watched Cora open the closet and stare at her clothing choices.

"Less than five minutes." Cora glanced at Addy over her shoulder.

"Five—shit!" Addy rushed to the window. She lifted it, careful to not use her shifter strength and break the glass. "Jatix!"

Jatix jogged down the porch stairs and turned around in the yard to look up at her. Decker was nowhere in sight.

"What's wrong?" Jatix asked. "Is she awake?"

"Yes. Cora says that he will be here in less than—"

She was cut off by a deafening crackle of thunder. Her eyes were drawn to the sky that at once was blue and clear. It was growing dark as she stared at it. A bolt of lightning streaked across the blackening sky.

"He's coming," Cora whispered.

Addy whipped around to find her mate changed into clothes that had not been in the closet.

Addy swallowed hard, rendered speechless.

Cora was one fierce-looking witch in black leather leggings, knee-high boots, and a matching leather tunic that molded to her torso. Her black hair flowed around her shoulders while her electric-blue eyes glowed.

"This ends today." Cora spun around and disappeared through the door.

Addy rushed out after her, racing down the short hall toward the stairs. She ran down them, not hearing any sound in the house.

What the hell?

Her family had been downstairs.

Addy arrived at the bottom of the stairs and paused.

Her father and brother were in the living room, watching television, but frozen in place. They had been yelling at the screen, watching baseball. The screen was paused. She glanced over to the kitchen, seeing her sister and mother standing in there, not moving.

Goosebumps skated across her skin.

Cora had done this.

"Oh my." Addy headed toward the foyer and found the front door open. She stepped out onto the porch, finding Kira standing on the bottom stair.

Cora stood in the middle of the yard, facing the direction of the incoming storm. Jatix and Decker were with her.

"What's wrong with my family?" Addy asked.

"Cora doesn't want them involved in this.

Come." Kira motioned for her to step away from the house.

Addy looked at her house. She had been right behind Cora. How had she done that so fast?

Cora threw her hand up. The air around her house shimmered. Addy blinked, and the door was now closed, and her house appeared as if no one was home.

The love she felt for Cora grew. She didn't think she could love her any more. This woman was protecting her family when it was her who was in danger.

Addy walked toward Cora with Kira joining her.

She stood next to Cora who turned to her with a small smile on her lips.

Here they were, going to face a pissed-off warlock. Three wolf shifters and two witches.

That's all they would need against one crazed warlock.

Right?

Chapter Seventeen

Cora stood poised, her muscles tight with tension. Her heart pulsed in her ears. She had never had a throw down with another witch before.

Tonight was the night.

Now that her body had rested, she was at full power.

She rotated her shoulders, the electric sensation coursing through her body and making its way to her fingertips.

Her parents were safe. That's all that mattered now.

Memories didn't lie.

She would no longer run from Derwin. She had thought all of this time that if she stayed away, he wouldn't hurt her parents if he still needed her.

But now the gloves were off.

If her parents were not in his clutches, and her mate was by her side, then she would face him.

End this.

Cora refused to live life looking over her shoulder.

Addy deserved more than that type of life. She wanted the world for her mate, and having to hide from Derwin was no life to live.

The rolling dark clouds came in above them. A flash of lightning struck across the sky.

Cora smirked. Derwin was trying to make an entrance.

She faced the woods at the edge of the dead-end street.

"He's in there," Cora announced, pointing in that direction. She sensed his energy.

"I've called in for backup," Jatix revealed.

"I'm texting them the location now," Decker said.

Cora gave a nod and walked down the street. Their home was about four houses away. Addy's family was safety tucked away inside. They wouldn't even know anything was different. She had put a protection spell around them as she had raced through the house. They hadn't even seen her come down the stairs.

"Don't do anything crazy," Addy said, walking alongside Cora.

"I won't. He wants the dark portal opened, he's going to get his wish."

"You can seriously open it?" Kira gasped and came up on her other side.

Cora didn't respond. Brumelda had taught her a great many things. Some she probably shouldn't have, but she had recognized the power in Cora and wanted to teach her all that she could.

They arrived at the edge of the woods. Cora stopped on her heel and spun to Addy. She gripped her arms and stared into her eyes.

"If things go haywire, I want you gone. Get away as far as you can," Cora demanded.

"What? No." Addy shook her head. Her fangs peeked through under her top lip. "I am not going anywhere."

"Promise me. I won't be able to deal if I know you are harmed in any way," Cora snapped. She stared into Addy's golden eyes and saw nothing but stubbornness glaring right back at her. "Kira."

She was desperate. She needed to know that

should she falter or fall, her mate would be protected.

"Don't worry, Cora. If I have to hog tie her myself, I'll get her out," Kira replied.

In the short time they had gotten to know each other, Cora was already considering Kira a friend. Kira would protect Addy. They were blood relatives, and the witch understood.

If something happened to Addy, Cora would lose her shit.

That would put everyone in danger.

Cora jerked her head in a nod, satisfied before turning back to the forest.

Thunder sounded again. The air around them was growing thick. Derwin was there. Not too far away.

Cora released her last hold on her magic.

She was now fully exposed.

"Damn, girl," Kira whispered, apparently affected by the rush of power that surged around them.

Cora forged forward, with Addy, Kira, Jatix, and Decker behind her.

She pushed out her senses, picking up Derwin and two other figures.

That's all he'd brought? Well, the wolves had

Rune, so he was down a man.

Derwin had clearly underestimated her if he thought he would be able to capture her with only a few men.

It didn't take them long to reach him. Cora held up a hand. She glanced over her shoulder.

"Wait for my signal."

Addy moved toward her, but Kira grabbed her by the arm. Cora met Kira's gaze and gave a slight nod of thanks.

She wanted to meet with Derwin first. Get a feel of what he had going on. She didn't want to reveal everything immediately. If he was as powerful as he claimed, then he would know there were others in the woods.

Cora turned back around and continued on. The woods opened to a small peaceful creek. The water rushed past. On the other side was the one man she had hoped to never see again.

"Cora. Cora. Look at you," Derwin quipped. The sarcasm dripped from his words.

"Derwin." She strode to the edge of the creek. It was wide, but the water level wasn't high enough that she couldn't walk through it. She rested hands on her hips and glared at him. "What do you want?"

"You have been a hard person to find." He cocked an eyebrow up, folding his hands in front of him. He was dressed as a standard coven priest. A long black robe with their coven's insignia on it, the hood was covering his head, only allowing his face to be seen. Two other guards stood off behind him.

She recognized them, Canton and Leif. They, too, had joined in the deceit of Derwin.

"And yet, you didn't get the hint," she said.

"Spunky, I like it." He grinned, marching forward to his edge of the creek.

The darkened sky was full of clouds. Lightning flashed again, and the winds blew swiftly, lifting her hair from her face.

"I just want to be left alone," she warned. She would at least try reasoning with him. "I don't want any trouble, Derwin."

"Then make this easy. Come back to Oceana with me. Rule with me." He held out his hand to her. He shook the hood off his head, narrowing his eyes on her. "Don't play coy with me, Cora. You know exactly what I want."

"The Oasis Moon was never a dark coven," she snapped. "We were peaceful, loving—"

"We were weak. My aunt lived in a fantasy. While she skipped around with her head in the clouds, she didn't see what I saw," he growled. He took his hand back, forming a fist. "With me, we will be the strongest coven there is. We will use the energy of the dark realm and rule this one."

He was crazy. Derwin wasn't strong enough to wield magic from the dark realm. Brumelda had cautioned her when she was a child, that many wanted what the dark realm had to offer, but there was only a few who were strong enough to wield it.

Cora was one who could.

But she didn't want to have to use dark magic unless she had to; only for the good of their world would she.

"There is nothing going on right now that would require such magic," Cora said. She sensed eyes on her from behind. So far, he hadn't picked up that she wasn't alone. Hopefully with her stalling, backup would have arrived.

Not that she needed help, but just in case, she had to ensure the town would be safe.

"But why wait?" he argued. "We need to prepare. Someone needs to take the reins of this realm and offer protection. We wouldn't want to get caught with our pants down when the enemy presents itself."

"Oh, so you're going after dark magic for the

goodness of this realm?" she asked. She bit back a laugh. Derwin was truly delusional. He believed by taking control of this world, he was protecting everyone.

"Why not me?" he exploded. He stalked down the bank of the creek, stepping into the thick dirt.

Cora braced herself, her fingers tingling with her magic.

"I am the prime candidate," he said. "I was born for this. This wretched world needs to know I am the almighty warlock who will control it."

"You can't handle what would come from the dark realm," Cora scoffed. She was growing tired of his ranting. His ego had him believing this craziness. Derwin was dangerous. If he somehow were to get the portal open, then all hell would break loose. "You are weak, Derwin. A true wielder of power would have been gifted the ability to open the portal themselves. Not someone who would have to hunt down a person who could."

Derwin paused, his face contorting to reveal his rage. A roar erupted from him. His hands rose swiftly, sending a powerful bolt of orange energy toward her.

Cora threw up her hands, blocking his bolt with

an invisible shield. The energy bolt ricocheted off her energy field and zipped up into the air.

"Get her!" Derwin ordered.

Canton and Leif sped forward, reaching the water. They hurried across. Cora backed away, knowing she would not be able to physically fight them off.

At that moment, growls echoed from behind her. Cora's head whipped around to see five wolves breaking through the woods, racing toward her.

Leif and Caton paused, shock registering on their faces before they spun to run back.

"Wolves?" Derwin backed up the bank. He scrambled back to the other side.

Cora couldn't let Derwin get away. He was too dangerous to be loose on the streets. If he didn't use her, he would find some other witch who would open the portal.

She hurried down the embankment and trudged through the water, glad she had conjured high leather boots for her feet. She crawled up the small hill until she was on the other side.

The wolves had no trouble racing through the water and passing her.

Derwin and his men were on the run.

"Fight them. I order you!" Derwin shouted.

Caton and Leif halted, and faced the wolves. Cora glanced at the beasts and cursed seeing Addy's auburn animal racing behind the others.

Cora rushed through the melee. Her eyes were on Derwin who was running into the other part of the woods.

The four wolves converged on the two warlock guards, surrounding them. Cora had to focus on Derwin. The wolves would be able to handle two warlocks.

Derwin darted into the woods.

Cora released a curse but pushed. She hit the trees and paused.

"Don't run now!" Cora shouted. She needed to draw him out.

"You think those wolves are strong enough to take me down?" His voice echoed somewhere off in the distance.

Cora made her way through the thickness.

"I know they aren't." She cackled. A snapping sound had her spinning in the direction of the noise. "But I am."

"You know nothing of true magic, girl. Those spells my aunt taught you were child's play."

Cora headed in the direction of his voice. She used her magic, allowing her to get a lock on his position. She lifted her hands before her in a defensive move that she'd been taught.

Child's play spells?

If that was what he thought his aunt had taught her, then he was sorely mistaken. Yes, all witches knew common spells, practiced what their ancestors passed down, but Cora had been born to a different breed of witchcraft.

Brumelda had known that and ensured Cora was well-versed in her magic.

"Well, reveal yourself now, so I can show you what your aunt taught me," she taunted him. She crept through the thick brush. Her hands warmed from her energy waiting to be used.

"You were to be a vessel, for me to use your power to open the portal," Derwin snapped. "Give yourself to me. Stop playing these games, and I'll take it easy on you."

Cora spun to where Derwin appeared.

"Not a chance." She scowled.

"Very well then. You made a mistake in following me here."

Vines from the foliage on the ground suddenly moved, sliding up her legs. They wrapped tightly around her, holding her in place.

"You don't want to do this," she gasped.

His demonic chuckle sent a chill down her spine. The vines crawled up higher on her. Her arms were snatched back by others.

"You aren't as strong as you think," he retorted.

Cora played the role of trapped witch. The vines tightened around her legs and arms. She glared at him as he drew closer. Her arms were brought behind her, the vines weaving themselves into handcuffs.

A growl sounded near her.

Goddess, please don't let it be Addy.

Cora's head jerked toward the sound.

A lump formed in her throat.

Addy.

The dark-auburn wolf made her way toward them. Panic gripped Cora. She hadn't wanted Addy near Derwin.

"Aww...your mate coming to save you." Derwin eyed the wolf. A devilish smile spread across his lips. "Glad she could join the party. She'll have to watch me use you until there is no more power left."

He was going to drain her?

Her gaze locked on Derwin.

"Leave her out of this," she pleaded. Cora needed to get his attention back to her.

"Oh, no. I want her to watch what will happen

to you. These mangy mutts will learn today who is in charge. Once I have the powers of the dark realm, then they, too, will bow down to me."

Addy didn't like the sound of that. She lunged toward Derwin.

"Addy, no!" Cora screamed.

Time appeared to slow as Addy's body was midair just as Derwin's orange bolt of energy struck her.

Cora's scream pierced the air.

Addy flew back, slamming into a wide tree trunk, landing on the ground, unmoving.

Cora found herself unable to stop. The sound flowing from her mouth increased in decibels.

The vines holding her untied and slid down off her.

She broke free from her restraints.

Her chest rose and fell quickly. She could barely bring in air. Her gaze focused on Derwin.

A read haze took over her sight.

"Yes, come to me." Derwin barked a laugh.

"You want the dark portal open, I'll do it for you." Cora's voice was unlike anything she had ever heard. She stood, lifting her hands, her body overcome with her energy.

Words of the ancients flew from her mouth.

The language was foreign but came to her. The air grew thick with magic. Her powers flowed through her, racing down her arms. She directed everything she had to the space next to him.

Derwin's laughter grew as he looked at the area where a ripple in the air near him formed into a dark hole floating in the sky.

"Yes!" he yelled.

Cora continued speaking the language of her ancestors. The black circle grew, an air current passing back and forth between the two realms.

Derwin faced the portal, taking his attention from her. He raised his hands, prepared to pull magic from the other realm.

Cora held the portal open, one hand controlling it.

"You wanted the dark realm," she rasped, her fingertips growing hot. The amount of electric current racing through her was more than she was used to.

The memory of Addy's wolf flying back and crashing into the tree flared.

She reached down within and used her free hand to direct energy at Derwin.

"What?" His head whipped toward her just as she swung her arm. An invisible force slammed into him, pushing him into the void. His screams echoed through the air before they were silenced.

Cora brought her hands together, closing the portal. She fell backwards, out of breath. The ground rushed up to her before she knew it. She landed with a thud.

"Ow..." she groaned. Her body felt as if she were hit with a Mack truck. She lay there, trying to catch her breath. It was over. Derwin was gone from this realm. He would pay for his deceit.

He had thought she'd opened the dark realm where the strongest of magic was cultivated.

No, she'd opened the realm to the Underworld.

Wait until he realized he was sent to the realm of Lucifer and his demons.

Addy.

She pushed up off the ground, turning toward Addy. She stood and stumbled to where Addy was now curled up into a ball in her human form.

"Addy," she whispered.

Please, Goddess. Let her be okay.

She reached Addy and knelt by her. Addy's red hair was matted to her face, sweat lining her skin. Cora placed her two fingers along the column of Addy's neck.

A strong pulse.

Thank goddess.

"Addy, babe. Can you hear me?" The scent of burnt hair and flesh surrounded her. Cora rolled her over onto her back, and it was then she saw the burn mark on her side where Derwin's energy had hit her.

Addy moaned. Her eyes fluttered before opening. Her golden gaze was out of focus.

Footsteps headed toward them. Cora put herself in front of Addy, unsure who was coming. It wasn't until a wolf appeared that she relaxed. The air shimmered around the animal as he shifted back to his human form.

Jatix.

"What happened?" Jatix asked, his gaze landing on Addy.

"Derwin," Cora replied. She turned back to Addy, brushing her hair away from her face. She had to advert her eyes from his nakedness. She would have to get used to shifters changing and not caring about their naked bodies. Back in Oceana, she had known shifters but wasn't around them much when they'd changed.

"Where is he?" Jatix asked, looking around. His hands were clenched into tight fists.

"We won't have to worry about him any

longer," Cora said. She met his gaze. "He wanted me to open a portal, and I did. Sent him straight to the Underworld."

"It's over?" Addy asked. Her voice was raw and husky.

Cora looked down at her mate and smiled. Unshed tears blurred her vision.

"Yes, it's over." She bent down and placed a kiss on her forehead. Now she would be able to live life, enjoy her mate, and search for her parents.

"Come on. Let's get her checked out by the healer." Jatix leaned down and picked Addy up.

"I can walk," Addy protested.

"Let him carry you," Cora pleaded. "You are injured."

"I'll be fine," Addy muttered.

Jatix continued on with Addy toward the creek.

Cora glanced behind her at the area where she had opened the portal. She exhaled. Relief filled her. She had no regrets about where she'd sent Derwin.

The Underworld was still too good a place for him.

"Cora?" Addy's weak voice called her.

She turned around and jogged toward her future.

Chapter Eighteen

"How do you feel?" Cora asked Addy. Her wolf came to stand beside her, pushing her head against Cora's legs. Cora laughed, rubbing Addy's head. Her auburn hair was thick and luscious. Cora was always amazed at how soft her animal's fur was.

Addy snorted before moving away from Cora.

It was a warm sunny day, and they were enjoying the outdoors. They'd left the woods and walked across their back yard toward their home.

It had been a week since her confrontation with Derwin. The wolves had apprehended the other warlock guards. The alpha and the beta of the pack had arrived, and they had everything under control by the time Cora, Addy, and Jatix had returned to them.

The three warlock guards would stand trial in Howling Valley. According to Evan, the alpha, his word was law. The three guards would be able to beg for forgiveness and their lives.

But at this point, Cora didn't care.

Now that Derwin was gone, the Oasis Moon would have to rebuild. She'd been in contact with her friend, Topaz, who said the town was relieved to hear that Derwin was no longer in this realm.

Cora had shared with her friend the events so they could start rebuilding. The coven would still be in chaos while they purged all of those who had sided with Derwin.

Including her brother.

She was still in awe that her own brother, her blood, had turned against her. Marden was set for trial in a month.

Cora wasn't sure if she was going to go to bear witness to his punishment for his hand in Derwin's conspiracy.

All of those who'd sided with Derwin would be tried for treason against their own kind.

Cora breathed in deeply, loving the scent of the outdoors. Fresh, free air had never smelled so good.

A month ago, she had been living in fear. Now she was a free woman to do as she pleased, a mate at her side and a place she could call home.

Now the only thing that was on her mind was finding her parents. She prayed to the goddess above daily for their safety.

"Are you going to give me back my Addy or not?" Cora joked with Addy's wolf.

Sometimes Addy's beast wanted to spend time with her, which she was okay with. It was nice getting to know both sides of her mate.

Addy gracefully took the stairs of the back porch and stood at the top. The air around her shimmered as she shifted. Cora watched, always amazed how her body was able to switch from animal to human. The fur withdrew into her skin, her bones contorted, and within moments, Addy was kneeling.

Her golden eyes met Cora's. A smile graced her lips.

Happiness filled Cora.

"There's my other Addy," she murmured. She walked up the stairs, straddling Addy's lap. She brushed Addy's wild hair away from her face. "I missed you."

"You've been with me for the past few hours."

Addy laughed. "You better be careful of what you say, my wolf will be insulted."

"I love your wolf. She's the best animal in all of Howling Valley." Cora grinned, dropping a kiss on Addy's lips.

"She recognizes mockery." Addy snorted.

"But it's the truth. She's definitely my favorite wolf." Cora pressed another kiss to Addy's mouth.

"We better be your only wolf," Addy growled. She pulled Cora close and covered her lips with hers.

Cora immediately opened her mouth to allow Addy's tongue to enter. She stroked it with hers. Cora moaned, loving how Addy kissed her.

It took her breath away. Slow, sensual, and full of her feelings.

Addy always shared and showed Cora how much she loved her. Cora tightened her arms around Addy's neck.

There was no room between them. Their breasts were crushed against each other.

Addy tore her mouth from Cora's. They stared at each other, both of them panting.

"You have too many clothes on," Addy said. Her gaze dropped down to Cora's tank and long skirt.

"Really?" Cora feigned surprised. Her core clenched with need at the feral glint in Addy's eyes. She rested the back of her hand on her forehead. "Oh, what shall we do about this monstrosity?"

Addy grinned, her hand half shifting to allow her claws to come through. She carefully ran her hand down Cora's shirt, tearing her shirt and bra into pieces.

"Hey." Cora laughed. She hopped off Addy and stepped away. "I can get my skirt. I like this one."

She giggled, removing her skirt and panties, settling back onto Addy's lap. They were in their backyard, and no one would see them thanks to the privacy fences lining the yards.

The sex between Addy and Cora was explosive. It didn't matter where they were, Addy always found some way to have Cora on her back with her legs open so she could feast on her.

Not that Cora was complaining. She loved Addy so much and needed her just as much as Addy wanted her.

"You, ma'am, owe me about three shirts and three bras," Cora murmured.

Addy's warm hands slid along her waist to cup her ass.

"No problem, ma'am. We can go shopping whenever you want," Addy said. She leaned in, nuzzling her face into the crook of Cora's neck.

"I'm going to hold you to that," Cora said. "Your parents invited us over for dinner, and I want to look my best."

"You look your best naked." Addy nipped her neck gently.

"I am not going over there naked." Cora gasped.

After the confrontation with Derwin when they had arrived back at the house, she'd had to free them from the spell she had woven over them. They had freaked out at first, then settled after realizing that she and Addy were safe. It wasn't the way she wanted to officially meet them, but she had explained how she had to keep them safe.

Thankfully, Kira, who had remained back in the woods during the melee, had been able to help smooth things over.

Later that evening all was well, and Cora had been forgiven.

"We're shifters, Cora." Addy lifted her head, a grin plastered on her face. She spread her legs wide.

Cora gasped. The new position opened her to Addy, leaving Cora to balance on Addy's legs.

It put her at Addy's mercy.

Addy captured one of Cora's breasts and wrapped her lips around the nipple. Cora sighed, not wanting to argue with Addy. She was stubborn enough and would start a tiny fight about Cora being naked.

Even though Cora had to admit their make-up sex was always worth it.

Addy bathed her breast with her tongue before moving over to the other one. Cora's core was drenched. It never took her long to get aroused.

"The scent of your cunt is driving me crazy," Addy murmured against the soft mound. Her gaze flicked to Cora's then went back to her breasts. Addy drew her tongue along her sternum up to her neck, where she gently bit Cora. It was never hard enough to break skin, but enough to mark her.

"It's because of you," Cora admitted. She rested her hands on Addy's shoulders.

Addy's hand slid down along her torso and farther until she was able to reach the destination of Cora's pussy.

"Yes," Cora hissed. She threw her head back and waited for what she knew was coming. Addy's finger connected with her aching clitoris. "Addy."

"I want you screaming my name," Addy

growled. She drew small circles on Cora's swollen nub with her thumb. She dipped her finger into Cora's core, gathering her cream and drawing it to Cora's clit. "You are so fucking wet."

"Ah…" Cora sighed. Her hips moved in rhythm with Addy's thumb. She was needing a good, quick orgasm. She was sure this would just be a quickie before her mate dragged her into the house.

Her body was racked with tremors as Addy increased her pressure. She flicked Cora's nub, faster. Her grip on Cora's waist tightened.

Cora's hips quickened. She dug her nails into Addy's shoulders as she rode her hand.

"Goddess," Cora moaned.

Addy's fingers dipped back into her core, drawing more of her honey to her clit. Her fingers were pushing Cora to the sweet point.

"You're so beautiful," Addy crooned. She leaned forward, nipping Cora's neck again, soothing it with her tongue. "Come for me, love."

She pinched and tugged on Cora's clit.

Cora detonated.

Her cry echoed around them. Her body was racked with an intense sensation coursing through her. Her energy rushed from her, filling the air with an electric current.

Cora finally coasted down from her intense orgasm. Her head fell forward, a silly little grin on her lips. She opened her eyes and met the heated gaze of her mate.

"That was absolutely perfect," Addy murmured.

"I love you," Cora said.

"I love you, too."

A wealth of emotion filled Cora's chest. She leaned forward and pressed a hard kiss to Addy's lips. Wrapping her arms around Addy, she knew that she had found everything she wasn't searching for right here in Howling Valley.

Nothing was going to take that away from her.

Ever.

Epilogue

ONE MONTH LATER

Addy was giddy with excitement. She had wonderful news for her mate, but she was going to have to hold it in for just a few more moments.

They were finally celebrating their union. It had been over a month since Cora had eliminated Derwin. The pack had secured the warlocks, and their trial had come and gone. The alpha had found them guilty of every charge brought up against them. They were sentenced to five years in a highly guarded paranormal jail.

Addy and Cora were able to now get back on track as a newly mated couple.

Cora's brother had gone to trial, and he, too, was found guilty. From what Cora was told, he was sentenced to banishment from joining any coven. Apparently, there was some international witch's council that would ensure he never joined another.

Cora had taken the news well.

Addy hoped he never attempted to reach out to Cora. If he did, he was going to have the Nightstar pack to deal with.

Addy stood in the kitchen, gazing out in the back yard. They had family and friends over to help celebrate their union. Even some of the enforcers had stopped by for the celebration.

Zeff was out on grill duty while his pregnant mate sat out there with their mother. Junior ran around in the yard, trying to chase his Papa Biggs. Addy laughed at the sight of her father, a big strong man running from a five-year-old.

Bess was chilling with Nolan, her mate. She cradled her daughter, Lily, in her arms.

Today was a wonderful day.

Addy's cell phone buzzed from its spot on the counter. She picked it up and read the message.

Where are you?

She grinned and responded.

In the house. Come around to the back where everyone is.

She slid it into her back pocket and went outside

to join the party. Scanning the area, she found Cora speaking with Kira under the tree in the yard.

Those two were becoming fast friends. Kira had introduced Cora to the White Lotus, and her membership to the coven was under review. The vote would be held next weekend. Cora was nervous, but Addy was sure they would allow her to officially join the coven.

Addy jogged down the stairs and made her way over to Cora.

"Hey, there you are." Addy wrapped her arms around Cora's waist and brought her back against her. "I missed you."

"You just saw her." Kira rolled her eyes. Her lips were curled into a smile.

Addy playfully growled at her cousin.

"Cut it out, you two." Cora laughed. She rested her hand on Addy's and turned enough to press a kiss on her lips. "Where'd you disappear to?"

"The bathroom." The lie rolled over her tongue easily. She felt guilty for the little white lie, but she was sure she would be forgiven.

"I can cover for you on Tuesday if you want," Cora said to Kira.

"Great, that would allow me to run some

errands I need to get to over in Grove Hill," Kira said.

Addy's attention was drawn to the side door of the fence opening.

"Babe." Addy pressed a kiss on Cora's bare shoulder. "I have a surprise for you."

"Really?" Cora spun around in her arms. A wide grin was plastered on her face. Her mate sure loved surprises and gifts.

Addy vowed to always keep her mate happy, and this gift she had for her would probably never be topped.

"What is it?" Cora asked.

Addy slowly positioned Cora so she faced the fence where Griffin walked through with her gift in tow.

Cora froze. Her eyes widened, tears immediately falling to her face.

"Mom? Daddy?" Cora cried out. She took off running across the yard toward her parents.

Cora's mother, Lavender, was the spitting image of Cora. Dark hair, tanned skin, and big blue eyes. Her father, Dallan, was tall, muscular, with dark-brown hair.

Her parents wrapped her up in a hug.

Applause and cheers filled the air at the reunion.

"I don't know how you did it, but this is awesome, cuz." Kira patted her on the shoulder. She wiped her tears from her face. Kira was always a big sap.

"I have my resources." Addy made her way toward her mate and her parents. One of Addy's student's fathers was a paranormal investigator who was a specialist in missing persons. She was able to get him the information he needed, and he was able to track down the Latimers. They had been hiding in a small town of Rollark, Utah.

Addy stopped near Cora.

"How did you do this?" Cora spun around to Addy. Tears marred her face, but it was the look of happiness in her eyes and on her face that tugged at Addy's heart.

"It's long story." She grinned. It had been hard to get information from Cora without her becoming suspicious, but once she had, James had taken over and performed a miracle.

"Thank you." Cora threw herself at Addy. Her arms wrapped around Addy in a death hug.

Addy grinned and looked over Cora's shoulder. Both of their faces were wet from crying.

Cora pulled back slightly, keeping an arm around Addy. "Mom. Daddy. This is Addy, my soul mate."

"Hello, Mr. and Mrs. Latimer. It's so nice to meet you." Addy held out her hand, but Lavender brushed it aside.

"No handshakes. Come here." Lavender tugged her in for a tight hug. Her body was racked with sobs. "I can't thank you enough."

"Let me in on this hug." Dallan's large arms encircled them all, pulling in Cora, too.

Addy's eyes met Cora's. Her heart was filled with love for this woman, and she was glad she was able to give her the one thing she had longed for.

Her parents.

Now, all was right.

They could move on and live out their lives just as fate had wanted them to.

Dear Reader,

Thank you for taking the time to read my book! I hope you enjoyed reading Addy and Cora's story as much as I enjoyed writing it.

If you want me to continue this series, please say that in your review!

Love,
Ariel Marie

Moon Valley Shifters

A FF WOLF SHIFTER BOXSET

Three steamy stories of female shifters finding the mate destined for them. If you love sexy as sin, F/F wolf shifters paranormal romance stories, that will leave you breathless, then grab this hot box set!

Book 1 Lyric's Mate

Lyric moved to Moon Valley for a fresh start. A new town, a new home, and a new job was a dream come true. Finding that her new boss was her mate was totally unexpected. Will she be able to keep her wolf at bay?

Book 2 Meadow's Mate

Meadow, the new teacher in town had her eyes on the only female enforcer in the pack. Little did she know, the enforcer had Meadow in her sights. When a group of rogue wolves blows into town, will Sage be able to save her?

Book 3 Tuesday's Mate

Tuesday, the new accountant in town was setting up her new business in Moon Valley. Tuesday is entranced by Sunni, the coffee shop owner. Their wolves know they are meant for each other. But will Sunni and Tuesday listen to their beasts?

WARNING: These stories are sexy, fast-paced and will leave you begging for more.

Want to hear more from this tantalizing book?
Download it HERE now!

About the Author

Ariel Marie is an author who loves the paranormal, action and hot steamy romance. She combines all three in each and every one of her stories. For as long as she can remember, she has loved vampires, shifters and every creature you can think of. This even rolls over into her favorite movies. She loves a good action packed thriller! Throw a touch of the supernatural world in it and she's hooked!

She grew up in Cleveland, Ohio where she currently resides with her husband and three beautiful children.

For more information:
www.thearielmarie.com

Also by Ariel Marie

The Nightstar Shifters

Sailing With Her Wolf

Protecting Her Wolf

Sealed With A Bite

Blackclaw Alphas (Reverse Harem Series)

Fate of Four

Bearing Her Fate (TBD)

The Midnight Coven Brand

Forever Desired

Wicked Shadows

Paranormal Erotic Box Sets

Vampire Destiny (An Erotic Vampire Box Set)

Moon Valley Shifters Box Set (F/F Shifters)

The Dragon Curse Series (Ménage MFF Erotic Series)

The Dark Shadows Series

Princess

Toma

Phaelyn

Teague

Adrian

Nicu

Sassy Ever After World

Her Warrior Dragon

Her Fierce Dragon

Her Guardian Dragon (TBD)

Stand Alone Books

Dani's Return

A Faery's Kiss

Tiger Haven

Searching For His Mate

A Tiger's Gift

Stone Heart (The Gargoyle Protectors)

Saving Penny

A Beary Christmas

Howl for Me

Birthright

Return to Darkness

Red and the Alpha

Made in the USA
Las Vegas, NV
04 December 2022

61108013R00148